FLIGHT WITHOUT END

JOSEPH ROTH

Flight Without End

TRANSLATED BY DAVID LE VAY

in collaboration with Beatrice Musgrave

PETER OWEN · LONDON

ISBN 0 7206 0324 2

Translated from the German
Flucht ohne Ende

PETER OWEN LIMITED
73 Kenway Road London SW5 oRE

First British Commonwealth edition 1977
Die Flucht ohne Ende copyright 1927
© 1956 by Allert de Lange Amsterdam
This edition published by permission of
Verlag Kiepenheuer & Witsch Köln
English translation © Peter Owen Ltd 1977

Printed in Great Britain by
Bristol Typesetting Co Ltd
Barton Manor St Philips Bristol 2

FOREWORD

In what follows I tell the story of my friend, comrade and spiritual associate, Franz Tunda.

I follow in part his notes, in part his narrative.

I have invented nothing, made up nothing. The question of 'poetic invention' is no longer relevant. Observed fact is all that counts.

Paris, March 1927   Joseph Roth

I

Franz Tunda, first lieutenant in the Austrian Army, became a Russian prisoner of war in August 1916. He was taken to a camp a few versts north-east of Irkutsk. He succeeded in escaping with the help of a Siberian Pole. On the remote, isolated and dreary farm of this Pole, the officer remained until the spring of 1919.

Foresters stopped by at the Pole's, bear-hunters and fur-traders. Tunda had no need to fear pursuit. No one knew him. He was the son of an Austrian major and a Polish Jewess, born in the small Galician town of his father's garrison. He spoke Polish; he had served in a Galician regiment. It was easy for him to pass himself off as a younger brother of the Pole. The Pole's name was Baranowicz. Tunda called himself likewise.

He obtained false papers in the name of Baranowicz, was henceforth born in Lodz, had been invalided from the Russian Army in 1917 on account of an incurable and infectious eye disease, and was by occupation a fur-trader resident in Verchni Udinsk.

The Pole counted his words like pearls; a black beard reinforced his reserve. Thirty years earlier he had come to Siberia as a convict. Later, he stayed on of his own free will. He collaborated with a scientific expedition exploring the *taiga*, roamed in the forests for five years, then married a Chinese woman, became a Buddhist, stayed in a Chinese village as doctor and herbalist, had two children, lost both of them and his wife to the

6

plague, returned to the forests, lived by hunting and fur-trading, learned to recognize the tiger's tracks in the thickest grass, omens of storms in the erratic flight of birds, knew how to distinguish hail- from snow-clouds and snow- from rain-clouds, studied the habits of foresters, robbers and harmless travellers, loved his two dogs like brothers, and revered snakes and tigers. He volunteered to serve in the war, but made such a sinister impression on his comrades and officers in the barracks that they sent him back to his forests as a lunatic. Every year, in March, he visited the town. He bartered horns, hides, antlers for ammunition, tea, tobacco and spirits. He also took back a few newspapers so as to keep in touch with events, but believed neither the news nor the articles; he did not even trust the advertisements. For years he visited a particular brothel to see one Ekaterina Pavlovna, a redhead. If someone else was with the girl Baranowicz would wait, a patient admirer. The girl grew elderly, dyed her grey hairs, lost first one tooth, then another, then her dentures, too. Every year Barano-wicz had a shorter time to wait, until eventually he was the only one to visit Ekaterina. She began to love him, was consumed with yearning throughout the year, the late yearning of a late betrothed. Every year her tender-ness grew, her passion increased; an old woman, with shrivelled flesh, she enjoyed the first love of her life. Every year Baranowicz brought her the same Chinese necklaces and the little flutes he carved himself, on which he imitated the calls of birds.

In February 1918 Baranowicz lost the thumb of his left hand when he was carelessly sawing wood. It took six weeks to heal; in April the hunters were due to arrive from Vladivostok; he was unable to visit the town that year. Ekaterina waited in vain. Baranowicz sent her a letter by a hunter and comforted her. Instead of the Chinese pearls he sent her sables and a snake-skin and a bear's coat as a bedside rug. So it came about, in this most important of all years, that Tunda did not see a newspaper. Not until the spring of 1919 did he learn from Baranowicz on his return that the war was over.

It was a Friday. Tunda was washing the dishes in the kitchen, Baranowicz came through the door, the dogs were barking. Ice clattered on his black beard, a raven sat on the window-sill.

'It's peace, it's revolution!' said Baranowicz.

At that moment all was still in the kitchen. The clock in the next room struck three loud strokes. Franz Tunda put down the dishes gently and carefully on the bench. He did not want to disturb the silence. Probably, too, he was afraid the plates might break. His hands trembled.

'All the way back,' said Baranowicz, 'I wondered whether I should tell you. I'm really sorry that you'll be going home now. We shall probably never meet again, neither will you write to me.'

'I shan't forget you,' said Tunda.

'Don't be too sure!' said Baranowicz.

It was farewell.

II

Tunda wanted to reach the Ukraine, Shmerinka, where he had been captured, then the Austrian frontier-post at Podvoloczyska, and finally Vienna. He had no particular plan; the way ahead was uncertain, even tortuous.

He realized that it would take a long time. He had only one resolve : to avoid encountering either White or Red troops and not to get involved in the Revolution. He no longer had a home. His father had met his death as a colonel, his mother had been dead for many years. A brother was an orchestral conductor in a medium-sized German city.

In Vienna his fiancée, daughter of Hartmann, the pencil manufacturer, was expecting him. The first lieutenant knew no more about her than that she was beautiful, sensible, rich and blonde. These four qualities had made her a suitable bride.

She used to send him letters and liver pâté in the field, sometimes a pressed flower from Heiligen Kreuz. He would write to her every week on dark-blue field-post paper with a moistened indelible pencil – brief letters, terse factual reports, news bulletins.

He had heard nothing from her since his escape from the camp. But he did not doubt that she remained true to him and was waiting for him.

He did not question that she would wait for him until his return. But it seemed to him just as certain that she would cease to love him once he was standing before her in person. For when she had become engaged to him he had been an officer. The world's great troubles had lent him an air of beauty, the proximity of death had enhanced him, the shadow of the tomb had fallen across the living man, the cross on his breast had called to mind the Cross on the Hill. If one assumed a happy outcome, then, after the triumphal march of the victorious troops through the Ringstrasse, there would be waiting for him the golden collar of a major, the staff school, and the eventual rank of general, all to the sound of the soft drum-roll of the Radetzky March.

But for the moment Franz Tunda was a young man without a name, without importance, without rank, without title, without money and without occupation – homeless and stateless.

He had his old papers and a picture of his betrothed sewn up in his jacket. It seemed wiser to him to travel across Russia under the assumed name which was as familiar to him as his own. Once across the border he could again make use of his old papers.

Tunda felt the pasteboard on which his beautiful betrothed was portrayed firm and comforting against his heart. The picture was by the court photographers who supplied the fashion magazines with pictures of beautiful women. Fräulein Hartmann had appeared as the fiancée of the gallant first lieutenant in a series 'Brides of Our Heroes'; the journal had reached him just a week before his capture.

Tunda was able to take the cutting with the picture from his coat-pocket without difficulty whenever he felt inclined to contemplate his fiancée. He mourned for her already, even before seeing her again. He loved her twice over : as an ideal, and as one lost forever. He loved the heroism of his far and dangerous journeying. He loved the sacrifice which was necessary to reach his bride, and the futility of this sacrifice. All the heroism of his war years seemed childish to him in comparison with the undertaking he was now attempting. Alongside his despair grew the hope that through this perilous return journey he could once more become desirable as a husband. He was happy the whole way. If anyone had asked him whether this was due to hope or sadness, he would not have known. In the hearts of some men sorrow creates a greater exaltation than joy. Of all the tears one may have to choke back, the most precious are those that one has shed for oneself.

Tunda managed to steer clear of both White and Red troops. In a few months he traversed Siberia and a large part of European Russia, by train, on horseback and on foot. He reached the Ukraine. He did not concern himself with the victory or the overthrow of the Revolution. The sound of this word evoked faint images of barricades, mobs, and the history instructor at the Cadet School, Major Horvath. 'Barricades' conjured up overturned black school benches, piled on top of each other. 'Mob' could be equated with the crowd which used to mass behind the cordon of militia on Maundy Thursday. Of these people one saw only sweaty faces and crushed hats. They probably held stones in their hands. Such people engendered anarchy and were addicted to sloth.

Tunda sometimes remembered the guillotine, which Major Horvath always referred to as the guillotin, just as he used to say Pari, instead of Paris. The guillotine, of whose construction the Major had an expert knowledge and appreciation, was probably by now erected on the Stephansplatz, where the traffic of carriages and motor-cars was held up (as on New Year's Eve), and the heads of the leading families of the Empire were rolling as far as the Peterskirche and into the Jasomirgottstrasse. Things were the same in St Petersburg and Berlin. A revolution without the guillotine was as improbable as one without red flags. One sang The Internationale, a song which cadet Mohr had declaimed on Sunday afternoons, the day of the so-called *Schweinereien*, when Mohr used to exhibit pornographic postcards and sing socialist songs. The yard outside was empty, there was stillness and emptiness when you looked out of the window, you could hear the grass growing between the great paving-stones. A 'guillotin', even as it were with 'e' amputated, cut off, was something heroic, steel-blue, dripping with blood. Considered purely as an instrument, it seemed to Tunda more heroic than a machine-gun.

But Tunda himself did not take sides. He felt no sympathy for the Revolution; it had ruined his career and his life. No longer a member of the army, he was happy not to be forced to espouse any particular cause when he encountered the historical process. He was an Austrian. He was on his way to Vienna.

In September he reached Shmerinka. In the evening he went into the town, bought bread dearly for some of his last silver coins, and avoided political discussions. He had no desire to reveal that he was unfamiliar with the situation and that he had come from a distance.

He decided to travel on through the night.

It was clear and chill, almost wintry; the ground was still unfrozen, but not so the sky. Towards midnight he suddenly heard rifle-shots. A bullet struck the stick from his hand. He threw himself to the ground, a hoof-blow struck him in the back, he was seized, yanked upright, thrown across a saddle, attached to a horse like washing to a line. His back hurt, he lost consciousness in the gallop, his head was filled with blood, it threatened to spurt from his eyes. He awoke from his swoon and slept just where he hung. The next morning, when he was untied, he was still asleep; they gave him vinegar to smell, he opened his eyes and found himself lying on a sack in a hut, where an officer sat behind a table. Horses neighed loudly and cheerfully in front of the house, a cat sat at the window. Tunda was suspected of being a Bolshevik spy. 'Red dog!' the officer called him. The first lieutenant very quickly realized that it was unwise to speak Russian. He told the truth, identified himself as

Franz Tunda, admitted that he was trying to make his way home and that he held false papers. They did not believe him. He began to reach towards his breast to produce his proper papers. But then he felt the pressure of the photograph as a caution, a warning, so he did not legitimize himself; after all, it could not have helped him. He was fettered, shut up in a stable, saw the daylight through an aperture, saw a small group of stars scattered like white poppy-seed. Tunda thought of fresh pastry – he was an Austrian. After he had seen the stars a second time round he fainted again. He awoke in a flood of sunlight, was given water, bread and brandy, Red Guards stood round him; among them was a girl in trousers, two large tunic-pockets stuffed with papers hinted at a bosom.

'Who are you?' asked the girl.

She wrote down all that Tunda said.

She held out her hand to him. The Red Guards went outside, they left the door wide open, he could feel the glowing sun though it was pale and without power to burn. The girl was robust; she tried to drag Tunda to his feet and fell down herself.

He fell asleep in bright sunlight. Then he remained with the Reds.

III

Irene had really waited a long time. In the social stratum to which Fräulein Hartmann belonged, there is a conventional loyalty, love founded in convenience, chastity springing from lack of choice and a fastidious taste.

13

Irene's father, a manufacturer from the period when a man's honesty was reckoned in terms of the percentage he obtained on his wares, lost his factory as a result of those same scruples to which Irene had almost sacrificed her life. He could not make up his mind to use bad lead, even though the customers were not fussy. There is a mysterious and touching attachment to the quality of one's own merchandise, whose reliability reflects the character of their manufacturer, a loyalty to the product which resembles to some extent the patriotism of those people who make their own existence depend on the size, beauty and power of their fatherland. This patriotism manufacturers frequently share with the least of their office-workers, like the great patriotism of princes and corporals.

The old gentleman sprang from the period when quality was a matter of determination and money was still earned ethically. He had war contracts but no real notion of military life. Therefore he supplied our soldiers in the field with millions of the very best pencils, pencils which our soldiers used just as little as the wretched products of other war contractors. The manufacturer showed the door to a quartermaster who advised him to be less scrupulous with his products. Others kept their good material for better times.

When peace came the old man was left with only poor material, the value of which had in any case fallen. He disposed of it together with his factory, retired to a country district, made a few short excursions and finally the last long one to the central cemetery.

Irene, like most daughters of impoverished manufacturers, remained in a villa, with a dog and a lady of noble birth who received visits of condolence and sincerely mourned the old man, not because he had been close to her, but because he had died without ever having been so. Her path from housekeeper to mistress had been interrupted by death. Now she possessed the keys to cupboards which did not belong to her. She consoled herself with an exhaustive regard for the suffering Irene.

Moreover, the noble lady had been the go-between in her betrothal to Tunda. Irene had become engaged in order to demonstrate her independence; an engagement was almost the equivalent of coming of age. The fiancée of a serving officer in the war was *de facto* of age. In all probability the love which had developed on this basis would not have survived the attainment of legal majority, the end of the war, the Revolution, had Tunda returned. But missing persons have an irresistible charm. One may deceive someone who is not missing, a healthy man, a sick man, and under certain circumstances even a dead man. But one waits as long as is necessary for someone who has mysteriously disappeared.

A woman's love is inspired by various motives. Even waiting is one. She loves her own yearning and the substantial amount of time invested. Every women would despise herself for not loving the man she has waited for. Why, then, did Irene wait? Because the men on the spot are greatly inferior to those who are absent.

Moreover, she was choosy. She belonged to that generation of disillusioned upper middle-class girls whose naturally romantic disposition had been destroyed by the war. During the war these girls were in secondary schools, high schools, so-called finishing schools. In times of peace these are the breeding-grounds of illusions, of ideals and amorousness.

During the war education was neglected. Girls of all classes studied sick-nursing, current heroism and war communiqués in place of iambics. The women of this generation are as cynical as only those with much experience in love are. To them the obtuse, simple and barbaric nature of men is tedious. They already know in advance the despicable, eternal and unchanging modes of masculine courtship.

After the war Irene took a post in an office because by then it had become embarrassing not to work. She was one of those better office workers, who would be summoned by the chief himself rather than by his secretary. Thus one began to imagine that the world was topsy-turvy, that a general equality was now the rule. What had the world come to when the daughters of manufacturers had to reply to 'yours of the eighteenth inst.' in order to be able to wear better stockings! Such times were out of joint.

Irene waited (like many thousands of women) morning, noon and night for the postman. From time to time he brought an unimportant letter from the lawyer. Meanwhile she was accompanied by the sighs of the aristocratic lady, whose sympathy resembled a malicious gloating.

Irene was in contact with family friends from Trieste. They were an ancient family who had lived for decades by the manufacture of tiled stoves and plaster casts of classical statues. This family is responsible for most of the discus-throwers which stand under bell-jars on mahogany showcases. A branch of the Trieste family had – probably for business reasons – embraced the Irredentist cause, moved its office to Milan, and split away from that part of the family still loyal to the Hapsburgs. Never again did the two camps exchange wedding telegrams, so profound are the consequences patriotism can engender.

After the war relations were gradually resumed. As victory conduces to magnanimity, the Italian branch of the family began by extending its hand to the Austrian. There was a nephew who came from Milan to Vienna; and it was this man whom Irene eventually married.

He won her by gallantry. In those days this was a rare quality in German men – it still is today. He was unpretentious, lively, businesslike, he made money, and possessed the important and astute capacity of being at once mean and of making a woman unexpected and expensive gifts. His personal taste stood in startling contrast to his profession; his house did not contain a single one of the statues he manufactured.

Irene was delighted when she left the paternal villa and – for the first time in fifteen years – the noble lady.

As the dog accompanied the bridal pair, the housekeeper assumed part of his functions: she snarled at the postman.

Irene did not forget Tunda. Contrary to her good taste, she called her first child – it was a girl – Franziska.

IV

I have narrated how Tunda began to fight for the Revolution. It was an accident.

He did not forget his betrothed, but found himself no longer on the way to her but actually in the neighbourhood of Kiev and marching towards the Caucasus. He wore a red star; his boots were in shreds. He still did not know whether he was in love with this girl comrade. But one day when, following an ancient tradition, he declared his allegiance he was confronted with her opposition to such poetic nonsense and experienced the collapse of traditional laws.

'I shall never leave you,' said Franz Tunda.

'I shall get rid of you!' retorted the girl.

Her name was Natasha Alexandrovna. She was the daughter of a clockmaker and a peasant woman, had made an early marriage with a manufacturer of French perfumery and left him after a year. She was twenty-three years old. Her expression changed from time to time. Her arched forehead became creased, her thick short eyebrows moved close together, the fine skin of her nose became taut over the bone, her nostrils narrowed, her lips – usually round and half-open – pressed together like two bitter enemies, her neck reached out like a searching animal. Her pupils, usually brown and round, in thin gold circles, could become narrow green ovals between contracted lids like swords in their sheaths. She did not want to acknowledge her beauty, rebelled against herself, regarded her femininity as a reversion to bourgeois conceptions and the entire female sex as the unwarranted residue of a defeated expiring world. She was braver than the whole of the male troop with whom she fought. She did not realize that courage is a virtue in women and cowardice the prudence of men. Neither did she realize that all the men were her comrades only because they loved her. She was unaware that men are chaste and ashamed to betray their affection. She had taken none of them; she had not acknowledged the love of a single one because she was more bourgeois than she dared to admit to herself.

The men of her troop were sailors, workers, peasants, uneducated men of animal innocence. Tunda was the only man of bourgeois origin. She took him immediately. She did not accept that this was a significant relapse into bourgeois behaviour. She acknowledged his sexual parity, she ridiculed his bourgeois outlook. Out of these qualities she decided to make a revolutionary. She did not realize that she was able to succeed in this only because, though surrounded by all the others, she and he nevertheless lived on an isolated island and, despite their differing convictions, came to understand each other more quickly than anyone else.

Natasha Alexandrovna fell thoroughly in love with Tunda, in accordance with all the contested rules of love of the old world she denied. And so, when she said : 'I shall get rid of you,' she did not know she lied. Tunda began by swearing eternal love with the assurance of all the superficial men to whom many clever women have fallen prey. It was only the persistent, contrary and determined resistance of the woman and her self-conscious and – to him – inexplicably offhand refusal of all the delights of male seductiveness that made him fall in love for the first time in his life.

Only at this point did his betrothed recede into the distance, and the whole of his earlier life with her. His past was like a country abandoned for ever, the years he had spent there utterly meaningless. His fiancée's photograph was a souvenir like the picture postcard of a street one has once lived in, his former name on his genuine documents like an old out-of-date police registration form.

Natasha once saw the photograph of his fiancée and, although jealous, handed him back the picture in unconcerned fashion, saying :

'A good bourgeois type !'

It was as if she had been commenting on an antique pistol, properly constructed for its period but now completely superseded and quite unfit for use in modern revolutionary warfare.

How well she knew how to apportion the hours of their day, to combine comradeship with the delights of love, and love with the duties of combat!

'We are moving forward at eleven-thirty,' she said to Tunda. 'It's nine now. We eat till half-past, you draw the map for Andrej Pavlovich, you will be ready at ten, we can sleep together till eleven-thirty if you aren't afraid of being too tired by then.' 'It's all the same to me!' she added with faint scorn, convinced that she had once more demonstrated her masculine superiority.

She remained alert, monitoring her pleasure as a sentry monitors the noises of the night. Bodily love was a call of nature. Natasha elevated love almost to a revolutionary duty, so giving herself a clear conscience. Tunda had always pictured women soldiers like this. It was as if this woman had stepped out of a book, and he submitted to her existence, validated by literature, with admiration and the humble loyalty of a man who, following false conventions, sees in a resolute woman an exception and not the rule.

He was a revolutionary; he loved Natasha and the Revolution.

Natasha devoted many hours of the day to the 'political enlightenment' of himself and her people, and to giving Tunda special supplementary instruction because he understood less about the Revolution than the workers and sailors.

It was a long time before he gave up thinking of the word 'proletariat' in terms of Maundy Thursday. He was in mid-revolution and he still missed the barricades. Whenever his men — for he commanded them now — sang The Internationale, he sprang to his feet with the guilty conscience of a traitor, he cried Hurrah with the embarrassment of a stranger or guest who, on a chance visit, must join in the observance of some ceremonial. It was a long time before he was able to stop himself wincing when his companions called him 'comrade'. He himself preferred to call them by their names and, in the early days was suspect on account of this.

'We are in the first stage of the World Revolution,' said Natasha at each lesson. 'Men like you still belong to the old world but can render us good service. So we take you along with us. You are a traitor to the middle class to which you belong, so you are welcome to us. Maybe you can be made into a revolutionary but you will always be a bourgeois at heart. You were an officer, the deadliest weapon in the hands of the ruling class, you have exploited the proletariat, you should have been exterminated. See, then, how magnanimous the proletariat can be! It acknowledges your understanding of tactics, it forgives you, it even allows itself to be led by you.'

'I lead it only for your sake, because I love you,' said the old-fashioned Tunda.

'Love! Love!' cried Natasha. "You can tell that to your fiancée! I despise your love. What is it? You can't even explain it. You've heard a word, read it in your lying books and poetry, in your family journals! Love! It's all been wonderfully laid out for you: here you have the dwelling-house, there's the factory or the delicatessen shop, over there the barracks with the brothel close by, and the summer-house in the middle. For you it's as if it were the most important thing in your world, you invest in it everything that is noble, fine, and tender in you and deposit your baseness in everything else. Your writers are either blind or corrupt, they believe in your architecture, they write about feelings instead of affairs, about the heart instead of money, they describe the costly pictures on the walls and not the accounts in the banks.'

'I've only read detective stories,' interpolated Tunda timidly.

'Yes, detective stories! Where the police come out on top and the burglar is caught, or where the burglar is the winner simply because he is a gentleman and pleases the ladies and wears a frock-coat. If you're only with us because of me I'd shoot you,' said Natasha.

'Yes, only because of you!' said Tunda.

She sighed and suffered him to live.

It is is unimportant whether anyone becomes a revolutionary through lectures, reflection, experience or through love. One day they marched into a village in the province of Samara. A priest and five peasants who were accused of having tortured Red Army men to death were brought before Tunda. He ordered the priest and the five peasants to be tied up and shot. Their corpses he left as a warning. He hated even the dead. He took personal revenge on them. This was taken for granted; none of the band were surprised at it.

Did it not surprise them that a man could kill without wanting to do so?

'You did it for me,' said Natasha scornfully.

For the first time, however, Tunda had not done something for Natasha's sake. As she reproached him it occurred to him that he had not been thinking of her at all. But he did not admit it.

'Of course it was for you!' he lied.

She rejoiced and despised him.

He would have shot all his comrades from the Cadet

22

School and from his regiment in the name of the Revolution. One day a political commissar was allocated to the section, a Jew who had adopted the name of Nirunov, a writer who rapidly turned out newspapers and proclamations, who delivered inflammatory speeches before an attack, and whose clumsiness in conversation equalled his ability to inspire. This man, ugly, short-sighted, foolish, fell in love with Natasha, who treated him as a political equal. Tunda wanted to be able to speak just like the commissar, he emulated him. He adopted the politician's technical expressions, he learned them by heart with the facility of a man in love. One day the commissar was wounded and had to be left behind; after that it was Tunda who delivered the political addresses and issued the proclamations.

He fought in the Ukraine and on the Volga; he moved into the mountains of the Caucasus and marched back to the Urals. His band melted away, he found reinforcements, he recruited peasants, shot traitors and deserters and spies, infiltrated the enemy's rear, spent several days in a town occupied by the Whites, was arrested, escaped. He loved the Revolution and Natasha like a knight, he got to know marshes, fever, cholera, hunger, typhus, barracks without medicaments, the taste of mouldy bread. He quenched his thirst with blood, he knew the pain of burning frost, of freezing in the pitiless nights, the languor of hot days, once in Kazan he heard Trotsky speak, the hard factual speech of the Revolution, he loved the people. He remembered his former world now and again as one remembers an old garment, he called himself Baranowicz, he was a revolutionary. He hated the rich peasants, the foreign armies who helped the White Guards, he hated the generals who fought against the Reds. His comrades began to love him.

V

He witnessed the victory of the Revolution.

The house in the towns displayed red flags and the women red kerchiefs. They moved about like living poppies. And the unknown Reds ruled — over the misery of the beggars and the homeless, over the ruined streets, the shot-riddled houses, the rubble in the public places, the wreckage that smelled of burning, the rooms where the sick lay, the cemeteries where graves were incessantly opened and closed, the groaning bourgeoisie who were compelled to shovel snow and clear the pavements. In the forests the faint echoes of the last shots died away. The last glow of fires flickered over the night horizons. The church-bells, ponderous or light, did not cease to sound. The wheels of the type-setting and printing machines began to turn; they were the mills of the Revolution. In a thousand squares orators addressed the people. The Red Guards marched in ragged clothes and torn boots and sang. The ruins sang. Joyfully the new-born emerged from their mothers' wombs.

Tunda came to Moscow. He would have found it helpful, in those days when official appointments abounded, to obtain a desk and a chair. He needed only to apply. He did not do so. He listened to all the speeches, visited all the clubs, conversed with all and sundry, went to all the museums and read all the books he could get hold of. He lived at that time by writing articles for the newspapers and periodicals. There was one platitude for protests and proclamations, another for sketches and reminiscences, a third for indignation and accusation. His own sentiments were more revolutionary than these facile speeches, which he used only as a tool. Writers experience everything in terms of language, no experience is authentic if it cannot be formulated. Tunda sought enduring, well-tried and reliable definitions in order not to be swept away by his own experiences. Like a drowning man, he reached with outstretched arms towards the nearest rock. Tunda, who had joined the army in the year 1914 and had marched through the Ringstrasse in Vienna to the sound of the Radetzky March a few months later, stumbled in the torn, haphazard uniform of a Red Army man through the streets of Moscow, finding no other outlet for his emotion than the modified text of the Internationale. Now there are moments in the lives of peoples, classes, individuals, moments in which the commonplace nature of a hymn is justified by the solemnity with which it is sung. But the professional authors were no match for the victory of The Russian Revolution. All made cheap borrowings and contributed well-worn phrases to posterity. Tunda was quite unaware of the tawdriness of these words; they seemed to him as magnificent as the times in which he lived, as the victory he had fought for.

He met Natasha only at night.

They occupied a bed in a room used by three families and cooked for themselves with the help of a spirit-stove heated by petroleum. A curtain patched together out of three blue and white striped skirts served for a wall, a door, and a window. Tunda, like all men a slave to the habit known as love, rebelled doubly against the conditions Natasha had laid down by becoming jealous. He loudly upbraided Natasha in the harmless manner of naïve men who think it is enough not to be seen in order not to be heard either. Moreover, the neighbours – who had gradually lost their curiosity in these conditions of proximity, much as a prisoner serving a life sentence gradually loses his eyesight – did not object to the substance of Tunda's jealous admonitions and complaints, but rather to the disturbance they caused.

Tunda wanted to know what Natasha did all day till midnight. Even had her principles allowed it, she would not have been able to list her activities, they were so numerous. She organized women's hostels, taught hygiene to midwives, supervised homeless children, lectured in factories where the work was interrupted so that she might interpret Marxism undisturbed, arranged revolutionary theatrical productions, conducted peasant women through museums, became absorbed in cultural propaganda, all without exchanging the wide riding-breeches in which she had fought for a skirt. She remained, as it were, a front-line fighter.

She met all Tunda's reproaches, she forestalled them with others which were more important in the context of the significance of the times.

'Why don't you work?' she scolded. 'You're resting on your laurels. We haven't gained victory yet, the war goes on, it breaks out afresh every day. The struggle against the bourgeoisie is over, but the much more important battle against illiteracy is just beginning. Today we wage a holy war for the enlightenment of our masses, for the electrification of the country, against neglect of children, for the hygiene of the working class. No sacrifice on our part is too great for the Revolution,' said Natasha, who had expressed herself with more originality in the field but could speak in no other fashion since her increased public activities.

'You talk of sacrifices,' retorted the naïve Tunda, who from time to time cultivated his own ideas about historical events. 'I have often meant to ask you whether you don't also agree with my views. I picture the period of capitalism as the period of sacrifice. Men have made sacrifices since the beginning of history. First they sacrificed children and cattle for victory, then daughters to prevent their fathers' downfall, sons to guarantee their mothers a comfortable old age; the devout offered candles for the salvation of the dead, soldiers sacrificed their lives for the Kaiser. Must we continue to make sacrifices for the Revolution? It seems to me that at last the time has come to cease making sacrifices. We own nothing, we have abolished property, haven't we? Our very lives don't belong to us any more. We are free. What we have belongs to everyone. Everyone takes from us what they think they need. We are not to be sacrificed and we make no sacrifices for the Revolution. We *are* the Revolution.'

'Bourgeois ideology,' said Natasha. 'No worker is going to fall for that. You say such extravagant things, I wonder where you get them from. You talk as if you have had at least six terms of philosophy. It's lucky that your articles aren't written like that. A few of them are quite good.'

Natasha showed less and less interest in love. Love now belonged to the conventions of the Civil War, the morals of the field, it was incompatible with peaceful cultural propaganda. Natasha would return home at midnight, their discussions would go on until two o'clock, and she had to be up again at seven; love would have made her daily work start an hour late.

She was also bored by Tunda, a man lacking in energy, whose decline into bourgeois ideology was evidenced by the strength of his interest in love. Nikita Kolohin, a Ukrainian communist, who fought for the national autonomy of the Ukraine and despised the Great Russians because they did not understand every word of the Ukrainian dialect, had recently begun to discuss the state of the Ukrainian nation with Natasha for hours at a stretch and had taken advantage of this opportunity to demonstrate how greatly superior he was to an Austrian officer. Natasha recalled that she herself had been born in Kiev, that she was therefore a true Ukrainian, that her place was in Kiev and only there. So she travelled with Nikita to Kiev – what else could she do?

She learned a few pithy Ukrainian expressions, travelled through the villages, awoke the peasants to their national obligations and joined up with Nikita again in Kharkov, which was no longer called Kharkov, and where a small room was available for Nikita and herself with friends.

Unfortunately, at the time, Natasha forgot to inform Tunda of her extended sojourn in the Ukraine. And this made Tunda jealous to begin with, for he assumed that one man, or several, were preventing Natasha from returning home at night. He sought her in all the clubs, all the hostels, all the editorial bureaux, all the offices. Then he grew melancholy; it was the first step to acceptance. He forgot to write articles, to earn money for the following day, he almost starved. He spoke of Natasha's absence to a few familiar comrades. They looked at him with indifference. Each of them had undergone similar experiences during these months. Was it not taken for granted that the world must be reconstructed anew and that minor private tribulations were trivialities?

Only Ivan Alexeievich, known as Ivan the Terrible,

because during the Civil War he had braided the long hair of captured priests, tied the braids together, and then forced them to run in different directions, Ivan Alexeievich who still served in the cavalry, was essentially good-natured and committed atrocities only out of an excess of fantasy, only Ivan permitted himself to engage in a long discussion about love.

'Love,' said Ivan, 'has nothing whatever to do with the Revolution. During the war you slept with Natasha, she was a soldier, you were a soldier, Revolution or no Revolution, Capitalism or Socialism, love only lasts a few years anyway. Natasha is no longer a soldier, she is a politician, and you are − I don't quite know what you are. In the old days one would have beaten a woman who didn't come home, but how can you beat this woman who has fought like twenty men? She not only has equal rights, she has more rights than you. That's why I never went back to my village where my wife lives with five children (unless she's had any more, but the first five are mine). Before I joined the Red Army I used to beat them all, all five and my wife too. Now I've been converted; if I were to go home I'd have to say to myself : 'Thrashing is out'. But it would go against the grain, I'd still want to thrash one or other of my family, and I wouldn't dare. And so conflicts would develop and there just couldn't be a decent family life if I had to control myself all the time.'

Even Natasha's return brought Tunda no consolation. She arrived after some weeks, had to see a doctor, and gave no more heed either to Tunda or to the Ukrainian state. She stayed in bed for a week; Tunda looked after the spirit stove. Anyone familiar with this activity will understand that it is calculated to drive even sentimental men to distraction. Tunda's love, which had given way to cooking, simply faded away during these eight days.

With the help of some old friends from the period of military communism he found a desk-job. He sat in the office of a newly-founded institute whose task it was to create new national cultures for some small peoples in the Caucasus by furnishing them with a new alphabet, primers and primitive newspapers. Tunda was commissioned to travel to the Caucasus with specimen newspapers, magazines and propaganda material, to the River Terek, on whose banks lived a small people which according to ancient statistics numbered some twelve thousand souls.

He lived for some weeks in the house of a relatively well-to-do Tartar, who practised hospitality on religious grounds and treated inconvenient strangers with friendly solicitude.

Little remained for Tunda to do. Some of the young folk had already taken control of culture, formed clubs and composed wall-newspapers.

It emerged that the people were not learning fast enough. They had to be helped with films. Tunda became the director of a cinema, which was however only able to operate three times a week.

Among his regular visitors was a girl called Alja, daughter of a Georgian father and a Tadzhik mother.

The girl lived with her uncle, a potter, who practised his vocation in the open air and with quite a marked talent, but who had also become somewhat stupid as a result of his monotonous existence. He was unable to converse and, to make himself understood, employed only a few fragmentary phrases which he seemed to extract slowly from his brain with the aid of his fingers.

The girl was beautiful and placid. She moved around

as if cloaked in silence. Many animals engender such a silence in which they then spend their lives, as if they had made a vow to serve some secret and elevated purpose. The girl was silent, her great brown eyes lay in dark blue pools, she walked as erect as if she carried a pitcher on her head, her hands lay always on her lap as if under an apron.

This girl was Tunda's second love.

VI

From time to time, Tunda's vocation took him to Moscow. Every night he visited the Red Square. The Red Square was silent, all the gates were closed, the sentries at the entrances to the Kremlin stood like wooden figures in their long cloaks, Lenin's mausoleum was black; up on the roof the red flag licked the sky, illuminated from below. Here was the only place where one still felt the Revolution, and midnight the only time when one dared to feel it.

Tunda thought of the Red War, of the years when one only knew how to die and in which life, the sun, the moon, the earth, the sky, were only the setting or the background for death. Death, red Death, strode day and night over the earth to magnificent marching music, with great drum-rolls which sounded like hooves galloping over iron and shattered glass, shards flew from its hands, the shots resounded like the shouts of marching masses.

Now this great red death had become the order of the day, it had become a quite ordinary death which

31

slunk from house to house like a beggar claiming its corpses as so much charity. They were buried in red coffins, choirs cast verses into the graves, the living went away and settled down again in their offices, wrote records and statistics, enrolment forms for new members and edicts against the excommunicated.

It is no solace to reflect that it is probably impossible to build a new world without desks and pens, without marble busts and revolutionarily draped shop-windows, without monuments and blotting-paper bearing Bebel's head as a handle; it is no solace, it is no help.

'But a Revolution never comes to grief,' said Kudrinski, a sailor who had been expelled from the Party, had commanded a warship for an entire year, and was now vainly looking for something to do.

He had met Tunda one night in the Red Square. One must suppose that Kudrinski, too, had come there to look at the red flag, the flag tossing on the Kremlin roof.

'A Revolution never comes to grief,' said Kudrinski. 'It has absolutely no bounds. The great ocean has no bounds; and a great fire – there must, somewhere be a great fire like this, as great, as boundless as the ocean, perhaps inside the earth, perhaps in the skies – a great fire has no bounds. The Revolution is like that. It has no body, its body is the flames if it is fire, or the flood if it is water. We ourselves are only drops in the water or sparks in the fire, without it we are nothing.'

Natasha lived in a requisitioned hotel. From six in the evening she applied herself to love – naturally of the sexual variety in which the heart, which belonged to the people, is not involved – explicitly irreproachable and hygienic love. No objection could be made to this from the standpoint of the equal rights of women. Comradeship was sacred to her. Since Tunda was no longer

32

eligible as a man, there was no occasion to despise him. He was merely, and more nearly, a comrade of equal status. How zealously she strove to help him! With what earnestness she strove in their discussions. But Tunda, when he was by her side, saw her as in a pallid mirror. He came to her as a man comes to a place where he has once been young. She was no longer herself; she was, as it were, merely the setting of her own earlier life. Natasha used to live here: so Tunda told himself whenever he looked at her. She wore a blue overall, she reminded one of a nurse, an overseer, a stewardess, but not a loved one and no longer a soldier of the Revolution. There even emanated from her a kind of chastity – although she needed love and had suffered its ravages – an inexplicable kind of arid virginity which is as typical of abandoned girls as it is of women who perform the act of love with intelligence and as a matter of principle. She lived in a narrow poorly-lit hotel room. Between a chair, on which lay tattered pamphlets, and the bed on which she performed for equal sexual rights, she stood as if on the bridge of a ship or on a speaker's platform, her hair combed straight back from her forehead, her lips compressed and no longer half-open as they had been when they had still kissed Tunda.

Tunda said to her:

'I can't go on listening to your lectures any longer; please stop! I remember how I used to love and admire you. I was very proud of you! During the war your voice was fresh, your lips were fresh, we lay together in the gloomy forest with death only half-an-hour away, our love was greater than the danger. I would never have believed that I could learn so quickly. You were always greater and stronger than I; suddenly you've become smaller and weaker. You are very miserable, Natasha! You can't live without war. You are beautiful only when fires are raging against the night sky.'

'Won't you ever get rid of your bourgeois ideas?' said Natasha. 'What fancies you have about women! Fires raging against the night sky! How romantic! I am a human being like you who happens to belong to another sex. It is much more important to run a hospital than to make love in fiery nights. We never understood each other, Comrade Tunda. The fact that we were once in love, as you call it, doesn't give you any right to shed faint-hearted tears over what I have become today. Better go and apply for admission to the Party. I've no more time! I'm waiting for Anna Nikolaievna, we've a report to write.'

It was Tunda's last encounter with Natasha.

She took a mirror from her brief-case and inspected her face. She saw two tears trickle slowly and evenly from her eyes, to the corners of her mouth. She was surprised that her eyes were crying although she herself felt nothing. The woman whom she saw crying in the mirror, was a stranger. Only when Anna Nikolaievna entered did it occur to her to wipe her face with her hand. She reflected quickly that it was more sensible not to hide one's tears. She planted her damp face opposite Anna's, like a threat or a shield or a proud admission.

'Why are you crying?' asked Anna.

'I'm crying because everything is so useless, so pointless,' said Natasha, as if she blamed something universal, which Anna Nikolaievna could never understand.

VII

I have already mentioned that Tunda was attracted to the quiet girl in the Caucasus named Alja, niece of the dunder-headed potter. Of all Tunda's actions and experiences which sometimes seem strange to me, the one I can most easily understand is his relationship with Alja. In the midst of Revolution, of historical and personal chaos, she lived like an emissary from another world, an ambassador from an unfamiliar power, cool and curious, probably as little capable of love as of intelligence, stupidity, good or evil, of all the earthly qualities which go to form a character. It was mere chance that she happened to have a human face and a human body! She betrayed no sign of emotion, of joy, anger or sorrow. Instead of laughing she showed her teeth, two white rows, neatly locked, a beautiful prison for any utterance. Instead of crying – she rarely wept – she allowed a few large bright tears to flow from wide-open eyes over a friendly placid face, tears which could not possibly be thought of as salty like all the common tears of this world. Instead of expressing a wish she indicated the desired object with her eyes; it seemed as if she was unable to long for anything outside her field of vision. Instead of refusal or rejection, she shook her head. She only displayed evidence of great agitation when, at the cinema, someone in front obstructed her view of the screen. In any case the surface of the screen was too small for her; she had to see every detail; she was probably more interested in the clothes of the characters or the impersonal matter of the furnishing of a room than in drama or catastrophe.

My description of Alja must be confined to conjecture. Even Tunda knew little more about her, though he lived with her for almost a year. That he came together with her seems obvious, as I have already said. He did not, alas, have what is described as an 'active temperament'. (However, it would be just as false to speak of his 'passivity'.) Alja received him like a quiet room. Having renounced all desire for exertion, struggle, excitement or even annoyance, he lived away from the main stream. He did not even have to be in love. He was spared even the minor domestic strategies. By day Alja helped her uncle, the potter. When evening came she slept with her man. There is no healthier life.

Meanwhile a deputy was appointed in Tunda's place. He himself had to go to Baku with his wife to make films for a scientific institute.

It seemed to him that the most important part of his life lay behind him. The time to give himself up to illusions was over. He had passed his thirtieth year. In the evenings he went down to the sea and listened to the sad scant music of the Turks. Every week he wrote to his Siberian friend, Baranowicz. During this period when they did not see each other, Baranowicz really became his brother. Tunda's name was not a fiction. Tunda was really Franz Baranowicz, citizen of the Soviet state, a contented official, married to a silent woman, resident in Baku. Perhaps his homeland and his earlier life returned to him sometimes in dreams.

VIII

Every evening there was to be seen in the harbour at
Baku, aloof from the cheerful brightly-clothed bustling
crowd, a man who in any other town would have excited
the interest of some people, but who passed unnoticed
here, cloaked in a deep and impenetrable solitude.
Sometimes he sat on the stone wall which bordered the
sea as if it were a garden, his feet dangling over the
Caspian, his eyes aimless. Only when a ship came in did
he evince any visible emotion. He pushed his way
through the dense throngs of bystanders and surveyed
the disembarking passengers. It must have seemed as if
he was expecting someone. But as soon as it was all
over – the Turkish porters returning to lean against the
white walls or play cards in groups, the empty cabs
rumbling off slowly, the occupied ones at a fiery rousing
pace – the solitary man went home in obvious satisfaction, not with the embarrassed expression we assume
when we have waited for someone in vain and have to
return home alone.

When ships arrived at Baku – and these were rare,
only Russian ones, from Astrakhan – excitement reigned
in the harbour. People knew perfectly well that no
foreign ships would put in, from England or from
America. But when the smoke was visible from a
distance people would behave as if they were uncertain
whether or not the ship might chance to be a foreign
one. For the same blue-white smoke-trails blow over
every steamer. Even when no steamer arrives, Baku

is in a ferment. Possibly it is due to the volcanic soil. From time to time there arises the dreaded wind which meets no resistance, which sweeps over the flat roofs, over the yellow landscape devoid of vegetation, dragging with it windows, stucco-work and shingle, which makes even the drilling-rigs, substitutes for trees in this part of the country, seem to sway.

Tunda used to go down to the harbour whenever ships arrived. Even though he knew they were only the antique local ferries bringing local officials and, rarely, foreign caviare traders, he would nevertheless always imagine that the ships might have come from some foreign sea or other. Ships are the only available means for such venturesome journeys. They do not even have to be steamers. Any ordinary boat, leisurely raft, or wretched fishing skiff could have attempted the waters of all the oceans. For those who stand on the shore, all seas are the same. Each small wave is sister to a large and dangerous one.

Alas, he had become resolved no longer to await the unexpected. His wife's reserve damped the noise of the world and slowed the passage of the hours. And yet he still escaped from his house, went down to the harbour, and was violently disturbed by the smell of this small sea. He would return home to see Alja sitting impassive at the window, watching the empty streets. She barely turned her head when he arrived and smiled if there was any sound in the room as if something cheerful had happened to her.

It was at this period that Tunda began to record every insignificant event, as if thereby they acquired a certain significance.

One day he wrote:

IX

Extract from Tunda's diary.

Yesterday, at half-past ten at night, the steamer *Grashdanin* arrived, three hours late. I stood by the harbour as usual and watched the crowd of porters. Many remarkably well-dressed persons arrived, first-class passengers. They were, as usual, Russian Nep-men* and some foreign traders. Since I began writing this diary I have taken a special interest in foreigners. Before, I never used to notice them. The majority come from Germany, only a few from America, some from Austria and the Balkan countries. I can easily tell them apart; many come to me at the Institute in search of information. (I am the only one in our Institute who can speak French and German.) I go to the harbour, assess the nationality of the foreigners and am delighted when I have guessed aright. I don't really know how I recognize them. I would find it difficult if I had to list the national characteristics. Perhaps I tell them by their clothing, not any single item of dress, but their entire bearing. Sometimes it is possible to confuse Germans and Englishmen, especially in the case of older men. Germans and Englishmen often have the same ruddy complexion. But the Germans have bald patches, the English usually thick white hair so that their ruddy faces

* Private trading and speculation was allowed for a short period after the Revolution under Lenin's New Economic Policy. (Tr.)

seem even darker. Their silver hair doesn't exactly inspire my respect. On the contrary, it seems at times as if the English grow old and grey out of dandyism. Their rosiness has something unnatural about it and – I don't know how to put it – something godless. They seem as unnatural as hunchbacks in strait-jackets. They walk around like advertisements for gymnastic apparatus and tennis-racquets, guarantees of a youthful old age.

On the other hand, many of the older men from the Continent look as if they were advertising office furniture and comfortable chairs. They grow wider from the hips downward; both their knees knock together; their arms are so close to their trunk that they appear to rest on soft, wide, leather chairbacks.

Yesterday there arrived three Europeans, whose country of origin I could not determine at first glance. They were a lady, a small, elderly, broad-shouldered man with a brown face and dark-grey beard, and a younger man, dark, of medium height, with bright eyes which were almost white in his dark-brown face, a very small mouth, and strikingly long legs in white linen trousers which hugged his knee-joints like a second skin.

The small bearded man was a little reminiscent of those coloured stone and plaster gnomes to be found among the flower beds in so many gardens. Somehow I found this gentleman's healthiness, the high-spirited brown face in its bearded setting, offensive. He walked beside the long-legged man and the tall lady with quick short steps, he almost skipped along beside them. It really gave the impression that he was an animal led by the lady on a slender lead. He made frisky movements, once he threw his soft, light-coloured hat in the air just before they climbed into the cab. Two porters followed them with trunks.

I think to myself that, at home, the movements of the bearded man must be slow and carefully studied. It is when travelling that he is lively. There was a lot of noise, and also they spoke so softly that I could not hear even though I strained towards them.

The lady in the middle was the first elegant woman I have seen since I returned from my last leave in Vienna.

They came to see me early today.

They are French. The gentleman is a Parisian lawyer and also writes for *Le Temps*. The lady is his wife, the young man his secretary. The young man is one of the few Frenchmen who understand Russian. It is probably for this reason, and on the lady's behalf, that he has come with them to Russia.

When the lady looked at me, I thought of Irene, of whom I have not thought for a long time now. Not that this lady was anything like my betrothed!

She is dark, very dark, her hair is almost blue. Her eyes are narrow, she looks at me with elegant short-sightedness. It is almost as if she did not care to look at me openly and directly. When she speaks to me, I always expect some command. But it does not occur to her to give me a command. I should probably be delighted if she were to condescend to give me some commissions.

At times she drums with the index, middle and ring fingers of one hand on a book, a chairback, the table. It is a slow drumming and a kind of rapid caress. Her nails are white and slender, bloodless nails; her lips, as if in deliberate contrast, are painted red.

She wears narrow grey shoes made of thin glove-leather, I could trace them with a pencil.

The secretary – whose name, according to his card, is Monsieur Edmond de V. – said to me :

'You don't speak French like a Slav. Are you Caucasian or Russian?'

I lied. I told him that my parents were immigrants and that I was born in Russia.

'We are spending three months in Russia,' said Monsieur de V. We have been to Leningrad, to Moscow, to Novgorod, the Volga, Astrakhan. In France we know so little about Russia. We imagine that Russia is in chaos. We are surprised by the general order, but also by the high cost of living. For the same money we could have explored all the French African colonies – if they were not so tedious.'

'Are you disillusioned then?' I asked.

The bearded lawyer threw a glance at his secretary. The lady looked straight ahead; she did not want to become involved in our conversation, even by a glance. I noticed that all three were disconcerted by my question. Perhaps they did not wholly believe in our public order. Possibly they took me for an informer.

'You have nothing to be afraid of. You can tell me what you think quite safely. I don't belong to the police. I make scientific films for our Institute.'

The lady threw me a rapid, narrow glance. I could not tell whether she was angry or whether she believed me.

(It occurs to me now that I may have disappointed her. Perhaps she liked me only as long as she was able to imagine that I hid some secret.)

However, Monsieur Edmond de V. spoke to me, with friendly eyes but with a disdainful mouth, so that I did not know which feature to trust. Monsieur de V. said:

'My dear sir, please don't imagine that we feel any anxiety. We are furnished with the best credentials, so that it is almost as if we were on an official mission. We would let you know if we felt disillusioned. No, we do not. We are delighted with the hospitality of your authorities, your people, your nation. We see only – I can speak for all of us – we see only the ethnological, the Russian aspects of what you postulate to be a fundamental social change. For us, Bolshevism is as Russian – forgive the comparison – as Tsarism. Besides – and here I find myself differing from my hosts – I have the hope that you will pour much water into your wine.'

'You probably mean,' I countered, 'wine into your water.'

'You exaggerate, my dear sir, I appreciate your civility.'

'Perhaps you are being provocative?' said the lady, and stared into space.

It was the first sentence she had addressed to me directly. Yet she did not look at me, as if she wanted to make it clear that, even when she spoke to me, she said nothing that was unequivocally for myself alone.

'I trust that you are joking and don't suspect . . .'

'It was a joke,' interrupted the lawyer. When he spoke he wagged his beard; I tried to decipher from its movements what he had said.

'Perhaps you may care to tell me something about France. It's seldom anyone comes here from your country. I know nothing about it.'

'It is difficult to describe France to a Russian unacquainted with Europe,' said the secretary, 'and especially difficult for us French. In any case, you would not gain an altogether accurate impression from our books and newspapers. What can I say? Paris is the capital of the world, Moscow may well become so one day. In addition, Paris is the only free city of the world. We have living among us reactionaries and revolutionaries, nationalists and internationalists, Germans, Englishmen, Chinese, Spaniards, Italians, we have no censorship, we have statutory education acts, upright judges – '

' – and an efficient police force,' I put in, because I knew this from the accounts of a number of communists.

'You've certainly nothing to complain about as far as your police are concerned,' said the lady. She still did not look at me.

'You have nothing to fear from our police,' opined the secretary. 'If you should ever wish to visit us, naturally not with hostile intentions, you can always count on me.'

'Absolutely,' asserted the beard.

'I shall come with the most peaceful intentions,' I affirmed. I realized how artless I must have looked. The lady looked at me. I regarded her thin red lips and said, awkwardly and childishly, for it seemed to me that I had to exaggerate my clumsy candour further : 'I should like to visit you – on account of your wife.'

'Ah, how charming you are !' exclaimed the beard very quickly. Perhaps he was afraid that his wife might say it. Notwithstanding, he could not prevent her from smiling.

I would willingly have said to her : ' I love you, Madame.'

She began to talk as if she were quite alone.

'I could never live in Russia. I need the asphalt of the boulevards, a *terrasse* in the Bois de Boulogne, the shop-windows of the Rue de la Paix.'

She fell silent as suddenly as she had begun. It was as if she had spilled a shower of fragrant glittering objects before me. It was for me to pick them up, to admire, to praise.

I looked at her for some minutes after she had stopped speaking. I remained expectant of further glories. I was really waiting for her voice. It was deep, penetrating and shrewd.

'One can't live anywhere as well as in Paris,' began the secretary again. 'I myself am a Belgian, so this is no local patriotism.'

'You are from Paris?' I asked the lady.

'From Paris; we would like to visit the petroleum fields this afternoon,' she said quickly.

'If you have no objection, I'll accompany you.'

'Then I would prefer to work and not go until tomorrow morning,' spoke the beard.

Before our appointment I ate in the vegetarian restaurant, as I was not hungry. Also, money was running out. My wages were not due for ten days. I was afraid that the lady might require a carriage – I might just be able to pay for it. But what if she asked for more? If she suddenly wanted to eat? I could hardly expect to be repaid by the secretary.

I ate without appetite. At half-past two I was standing in the scorching sunlight in front of the station.

After twenty minutes she arrived in a carriage, alone.

'You will have to travel just with me,' she said.

45

'We have decided to leave Monsieur de V. with my husband. He wants to wander around in the town and is afraid that he won't make himself understood.'

We sat among street-vendors, workers, half-veiled Mohammedan women, homeless boys, lame beggars, hawkers, white confectioners who sold oriental sweetmeats. I pointed out the drilling towers to her.

'How tedious,' she said.

We arrived at Sabuntschi.

I said: 'There's no point in looking at the town. It would be too tiring, it's hot. We must wait for the next train. We'll go back.'

We travelled back.

When we got out in Baku we were ashamed of ourselves. After some minutes we looked at each other simultaneously and laughed.

We drank soda-water in a small booth, buzzing with flies; a nauseating fly-paper hung at the window.

I became very hot though I drank water incessantly. I had nothing to say, the silence was even more oppressive than the heat. But she sat there, unaffected by the heat, the dust, the filth which surrounded us, and only occasionally repelled a fly.

'I love you,' I said – and, although I was already quite red from the heat, became even redder.

She nodded.

I kissed her hand. The soda-water seller regarded me with malice. We left.

I walked with her through the Asiatic old town. It was still broad daylight. I cursed it.

We wandered about for two hours. I was afraid that she would get tired or that we might encounter her husband and the secretary. We reached the sea for no special reason. We sat on the quay, I kissed her hand repeatedly.

Everyone looked at us. A few acquaintances greeted me.

Night fell quickly. We went into a small hotel; the owner, a Levantine Jew, recognized me. He thinks I am a man of influence and is probably glad to know something intimate about me. He has probably promised himself to make use of his secret sometime.

It was dark, we felt the bed, we could not see it.

'Something's stinging me,' she said later.

But we did not turn on the light.

I kissed her, her finger pointed now here, now there, her skin glowed in the dark, I pursued her dancing finger with trembling lips.

She got into a carriage, she will return tomorrow morning with her husband and the secretary. She will say goodbye. They are travelling to the Crimea, and then from Odessa to Marseilles.

I am writing this two hours after having made love to her. It seems to me that I must write it down so that tomorrow I shall still know that it really happened.

Alja has just gone to bed.

I don't love her any more. I find the quiet curiosity with which she has received me for months artful. She receives my love as a silent person submits to the tipsy or talkative . . .

They came next day to say goodbye to Tunda.

'I purposely detained Monsieur de V. yesterday,' said the lawyer. 'I am convinced that one cannot show two persons as much as one. According to what my wife told me yesterday, you must have seen a great many

47

interesting things.'

The lawyer really resembled a dwarf, though no longer the harmless kind standing on a green lawn but one dwelling among sinister rocks.

They made their farewells like strangers. 'Here,' said the lady before she left, giving Tunda a piece of paper with her address.

He did not read it till an hour had passed.

From that day on, Tunda realized that there was nothing left for him to do in Baku. The women we encounter excite our imagination rather than our hearts. We love the world they represent and the destiny they mark out for us.

What remained from the foreign woman's visit was her remark about the shop-windows of the Rue de la Paix. Tunda thought of the shop-windows of the Rue de la Paix as he looked out his old papers.

It was an open order, Number 253, with a round stamp, signed by Kreidl, Colonel, made out by Sergeant Palpiter. The yellow paper, frayed in its creases, had become a sort of sacrament; it was smooth, it felt like tallow and had the slipperiness of candles. Its purport was unmistakable. It stated that First Lieutenant Franz Tunda was to proceed to Lemberg for kitting out.

Had he not been taken prisoner a day later, this official journey would have become a small furtive spree to Vienna.

The name Franz Tunda stood there so large, so strong, so meticulously recorded, that it almost emerged from the surface of the document to assume a life of its own.

Names have their own kind of vitality, as do clothes. Tunda, who had been Baranowicz for several years, saw the real Tunda emerge from the document.

48

Next to the open order lay Irene's photograph. The pasteboard was crumpled, the portrait faded. It showed Irene in a dark, high-necked dress, a serious dress of the kind one puts on when being photographed for a warrior in the field. The expression was still lively, flirtatious and shrewd, an accomplished blending of natural talent and the retoucher's art.

While Tunda was looking at the picture he was thinking of the shop-windows of the Rue de la Paix.

X

One day there appeared at the Austrian Consulate in Moscow a stranger in a black leather jacket, in frayed shoes, with a stubbly beard on a brown and craggy face, with an old fur cap which looked older than it was because outside the first warm March sun was shining. The sunlight fell through two wide windows on the brown wooden barrier behind which sat an official; it shone on coloured brochures for the spas of Salzburg and the Tyrol. The stranger spoke with a faultless official dialect, the dialect of the Austrian better class which even tolerates many High German words if they are spoken melodiously, and at a distance sounds like a kind of nasal Italian. This dialect supported and confirmed the stranger's story better than any document would have done. And this story needed some confirmation, since it sounded improbable.

The stranger stated that he had arrived in a Siberian prisoner-of-war camp in the year 1916 as an Austrian first lieutenant. He had managed to escape from there.

From the day of his escape he lived in the Siberian forests with a hunter who owned a house on the edge of the *taiga*. Both men supported themselves by hunting. Eventually, one of them was overcome by homesickness. He started out without money. He travelled for six months. He could only cover short stretches by train. He still had an old document, an open order. It could be seen from this that the stranger's name was Franz Tunda, and that he had been a first lieutenant in the old Austrian Army. He had not lost his Austrian citizenship after the downfall of the Monarchy, because he carried on his father's business in Linz, in Upper Austria. A telegram to Linz with a prepaid reply confirmed the former officer's statements. The old class-registers of the Cadet School, which likewise corroborated the first lieutenant's assertions, were still preserved in the archives of the War Ministry in Vienna. The Consul's remaining doubts were dispelled by the likeable and frank manner of the stranger, who gave the impression that he had never lied in his life, and by the fact that the wily official could not credit a former officer with the intelligence required for a lie.

No statute existed under which anyone returning belatedly from Siberia could undertake a journey home at the expense of the frugal Austrian Government. However, there did exist a relief fund for 'special cases' and the Austrian Minister agreed – after some hesitation, which he owed more to his office than his conscience – that Tunda could be included under 'special cases'.

Tunda received an Austrian passport, an exit permit from the Russian Commissariat for Foreign Affairs through the mediation of the legation, and a travel pass to Vienna via Katowicz. It was all arranged more quickly than he had expected, so that he was not able to carry out his intention of travelling to Baku to say farewell to his wife. For he assumed that he would be under police supervision, and that his return home would be regarded as suspicious. He found himself in one of those situations in which one is compelled by external circumstances to commit an injustice knowingly and wilfully, even to aggravate it, in the face of one's own conscience. He was a wretch to leave a woman on her own; but he made himself still more despicable by not taking his leave of her in person. He merely wrote to her that he had to be away for some months. He enclosed some banknotes because he had doubts about sending a postal order. He even informed his wife of his brother's address, the *poste restante* at Irkutsk, if it should be required.

Then, one evening, he sat in a train travelling westward and felt as if he was not making this journey of his own free will. Things had turned out as they always had in his life, as indeed much that is important does in the lives of others, who are deceived by the more noisy and deliberate nature of their activities into believing that an element of self-determination governs their decisions and transactions. However, they forget that over and above their own brisk exertions lies the hand of fate.

On one of those fine April mornings, when the Inner City of Vienna is as joyful as it is elegant, on one of those mornings when beautiful women stroll along the Ringstrasse with leisured gentlemen, when dark-blue siphons shine on the bright café terraces and the Salvation Army organizes musical processions, Franz Tunda appeared on the crowded sunny side of the Graben* in

* One of Vienna's most elegant shopping and promenading streets. Trs.

the same garb in which he had presented himself at the consulate in Moscow, and created an undoubted sensation. To a chemist standing in front of his aromatic establishment on the corner, he looked like a 'Bolshevik'. Tunda's long legs seemed even longer because he was wearing riding-breeches and high soft knee-boots. They exuded a strong odour of leather. The fur cap sat low over his sullen eyes. The chemist read danger to his shop in this face.

So Tunda found himself in Vienna. He drew unemployment relief, lived wretchedly, and looked up a few of his old friends. They informed him that his fiancée was married, and probably living in Paris.

XI

At the end of April I received the following letter from Franz Tunda:

My dear Roth,

Last night I happened to come across your address. I have been home again for two months; I don't know whether the word 'home' is appropriate. For the time being I live on unemployment relief and am applying for a place as a clerk with the Vienna municipality. This is probably hopeless. Forty per cent of the inhabitants are looking for some sort of job. What's more – I frankly confess that I would be unhappy if I did obtain a position here.

You will naturally ask why I left Russia. I don't

know the answer. I am not even ashamed. I don't think there is anyone in the world who could tell you with a clearer conscience why he has or has not done this or that. I don't know whether I wouldn't go to Australia, America, China or back to Siberia, to my brother Baranowicz, tomorrow if I had the chance. I only know that I have not been driven by any so-called 'unrest'; on the contrary, I am totally calm. I have nothing to lose. I am neither filled with courage nor looking for adventure. I drift with the wind and I am not afraid of ruin.

I have a cold meal once a day and drink tea in a small working man's café.

I wear a blue *rubashka* and a grey cap and attract attention.

If you can, send me an old suit and a *new* hat. I stroll along the Ringstrasse at least three times a day, also along the Graben in the mornings, when the smart public take the air. Meanwhile I am growing a beard because I am already conspicuous anyhow.

Ten years ago I was one of the smart public myself. It was on my last leave. Fräulein Hartmann walked on my right, my sabre slapped against my left side. At that time all I wished for was to be transferred to the cavalry after the war. Old Herr Hartmann could have fixed it. Now he lies in the central cemetery. I visited his grave, out of piety and boredom. It is a so-called family vault. Violets bloom there eternally under a red lamp held by a winged boy. The inscription is dignified and simple, as Hartmann himself always was.

I hear that my fiancée has been married for only four years, so she must have waited for me quite a long time. Four years ago I might still possibly have made a husband for her.

But today – I think I have become very much of a stranger in this world.

You ask whether I felt at home in Russia?

During my last months there I lived in a state for which there is no name, either in Russian or German, probably in no language in the world, a state between resignation and expectation. I imagine that the dead find themselves temporarily in this situation, when they have abandoned the earthly life and have not yet begun the other. It seemed to me as if I had fulfilled a task, fulfilled it so completely, so thoroughly, that I no longer had the right to remain contemplating its inexorable completion. It seemed to me as if Baranowicz had perished and Tunda had yet to be born.

I lived in Baku with Alja, my Caucasian wife, in a state of endless preparation for nothing. My work consisted of making or commissioning photographic and cinematographic records of the life of the Caucasian peoples. I did not exert myself. But the administrative system of the Soviet state is large and extensive and intricate – a deliberate, skilled and very refined intricacy within which every individual is only a smaller or larger point, linked with the next larger point and with no notion of his significance in relation to the whole. In the streets, in the offices, you see nothing but such points, points that exist in a mysterious and important, in fact a very close, relationship to you; but what this relationship is you do not know. There exist several elevated points which are aware of all the relationships; they have a bird's eye view, as it were. But you yourself do not perceive that they are placed at a higher level. You do not know whether you will be left undisturbed in your place. It is possible that soon, at the very next moment, you will be removed — and not just from above, but, in a sense, by something emerging from the foundation on which you stand. Imagine a chessboard with the pieces not standing on it but stuck into it and manipulated by the hand of the player, who sits under the table.

You are not only left to fear and hope. You have duties and functions also. You have your idealism, there is room for personal ambition. At times you can even predict the success or failure of some enterprise. But in many cases what happens is contrary to all your expectations. For instance, you have entirely neglected some duty and anticipate a very unpleasant outcome. But what transpires is either nothing at all or something very pleasant. So you never know whether the unpleasant outcome has not become manifest in the guise of a pleasant one. You can trust neither your successes nor your failures.

The worst is that you are under constant surveillance, without knowing by whom. In the office where you work, someone is a member of the secret police. It may be the charwoman who scrubs the floor every week, or it may be the learned professor who is in process of drawing up an alphabet of the Tartar language. It may be the secretary to whom you dictate your letters, or the manager who deals with the supply of office equipment and the replacement of broken windows. They all, without exception, call you Comrade. You, too, call all of them Comrade. But you suspect each one of being a spy and realize at the same time that each takes you for a spy. You do not have a guilty conscience, you are a revolutionary, you are not afraid of being observed. But you fear that, at least, you may be taken for an informer. You are harmless, but because you must strive to appear so the others notice your endeavours. That in turn makes you anxious that they may no longer consider you harmless.

One needs steady nerves for this kind of existence, and a large quota of revolutionary zeal. For one must allow that the Revolution, surrounded as it is by declared enemies, has no other chance of maintaining its power than by sacrificing any individual when necessary. Imagine yourself lying on the altar for years without being slaughtered!

For all that, I would have stayed in Russia – at least, so I believe – if one day a party had not arrived from France, on a pleasure rather than a study trip, a lawyer and his wife and secretary. The secretary was the wife's lover, and the lawyer managed so to arrange matters that I spent a day alone with his wife and an unforgettable evening in a hotel. I was the tool of his revenge. When she left, the woman, who took me for a dangerous informer of the Tcheka, handed me a card on which she had written in a triumphant hand: 'So you are from the secret police after all!', after I had endeavoured to rid her of the absurd idea. For that was why she had slept with me.

That is by the way. What matters is that the arrival of these foreigners suddenly made it clear to me that I had yet to begin my life, even though I had already experienced so much. It was remarkable that as soon as I saw this lady I thought of my fiancée's name: Irene. I yearn for her. Perhaps because I cannot discover where she lives and to whom she is married, possibly because I know that she waited for me for a long time.

I believe that the foreign woman's arrival at Baku was more than fortuitous. It was as if someone had opened a door which I had always thought of, not as a door, but as part of the wall that surrounded me. I saw a way out and used it. Now I am outside and very much at a loss.

So this is your world! Again and again I marvel at its solidity. In Russia, when we were fighting for the Revolution, we thought we were fighting the world, and when we were victorious we thought that victory over the whole world was near. Even now, over there, they have no idea how firm this world is. I feel a stranger in it. It is as if I was protesting against it in saying it to you twice over. I go around with alien eyes, alien ears, an alien attitude to people. I meet old friends, acquaintances of my father, and find I have to make an effort to understand what they are saying to me.

I continue to play my part as a 'Siberian' just returned home. People ask about my experiences and I lie as best I can. To avoid contradicting myself, I have begun to write down everything I have invented during the last few weeks; it has grown into fifty large quarto pages, it amuses me to do this, I am fascinated by what I shall write next.

This has turned into a very long letter. You won't be surprised at this – it is a long time since we last spoke to each other. I greet you in the name of old friendship.

Franz Tunda.

XII

Why had he left Russia? Tunda might be labelled immoral and unprincipled. Men who have a clear sense of direction and a moral objective, as well as those who are ambitious, look different from my friend Tunda.

My friend was the very model of an unreliable character. He was so unreliable that no one could even accuse him of egoism.

He did not strive for so-called personal advantage. His ideas were as little egoistic as they were moralistic. If it were absolutely necessary to characterize him by some particular attribute, I would say that his most significant quality was the desire for freedom. For he was as willing to throw away his assets as he was able to avert what was of disadvantage. For the most part he behaved as the mood took him, occasionally from conviction, always from necessity. He possessed more vitality than the Revolution could dispose of at the time. He possessed more independence than can be utilized by any theory that endeavours to make life conform to it. Basically he was a European, an 'individualist', as educated people say. He required complex situations to enjoy life to the full. He needed an atmosphere of tangled falsehoods, false ideals, seeming health, arrested decay, red-painted ghosts, the atmosphere of cemeteries that look like ballrooms, or factories, or castles, or schools or drawing-rooms. He required the proximity of skyscrapers that always look as if they are about to topple and yet are certain to endure for centuries.

He was a 'modern man'.

Admittedly, he found the thought of his fiancée, Irene, enticing. If he had strayed somewhat from the path he had taken six years before, he now returned to it. Where did she live? How did she live? Did she love him? Had she waited for him? What would he be like today if he had reached her then?

I confess that, after reading Tunda's letter, these were the questions I considered first, rather than the more immediate one of how to help Tunda. I knew that he was one of those men to whom material security means absolutely nothing. He was never afraid of going under. He was never concerned about hunger, which determines almost all present-day human activities. It is a kind of talent for survival. I know a few men of this kind. They live like fish in water: always on the lookout for plunder, never in fear of destruction. They are proof against both wealth and poverty. They do not show the signs of deprivation; and they are thereby equipped with a hard-heartedness which allows them not to register the private needs of others. They are the greatest enemies of compassion and of the so-called social conscience.

They are therefore the natural enemies of society.

It did not occur to me to help Tunda till a week later. I sent him a suit and wondered whether I should not write to his brother, to whom Tunda had not spoken since he entered the Cadet School.

XIII

Tunda's brother George was an orchestral conductor in a medium-sized German city.

Franz himself should really have become a musician. But old Major Tunda failed to appreciate the musical gifts of his younger son. He was a soldier, for him a musician was a military bandmaster, a civilian functionary attached to the Army by an ordinary contract, always in the embarrassing position of being subject to dismissal with a meagre pension entitlement if things went wrong. The Major would have liked to have made one son into a civil servant, the other into an officer.

George fell down one day, broke his leg, and was to limp for the rest of his life. He was unable thereafter to attend school regularly. Franz had received some musical instruction and wanted to become a musician. But as his brother's illness was very expensive, and as the Major had in any case lost interest in George because of his infirmity, he decided that George should have the music lessons from then on.

On grounds of economy Franz entered the Cadet School.

In those days Franz hated his brother. He envied him the good fortune of having fallen and broken his leg. He wanted to quit the Cadet School at any price. He hoped that he too might fall over one day and break a leg or an arm. He did not worry about what would happen afterwards. At the very least he wished for heart-disease. He thought himself very crafty. But the outcome of his exertions was the delight of his teachers and his father and excellent prospects for a military career.

The greater his success at the Cadet School, the stronger grew his hatred for his brother. Meanwhile George studied at the musical academy. Both brothers had to go home for the Christmas and Easter holidays. They slept in the same room, ate at the same table, and did not say a word to each other. They differed markedly in outward appearance. Franz took after his father, George after his mother. It is possible that it was because of his infirmity and the necessity to keep to his room, because of solitude and introspection and pre-occupation with books, that he acquired the melancholy expression which is characteristic of so many Jews and sometimes gives them a superior air. But Franz, because of his mode of life, was able to suppress any tragic pre-disposition which he might have inherited from his Jewish mother. Moreover, I am prepared to concede that a man's occupation may have a greater influence on his features than his race. (I have even seen anti-semitic librarians who might easily have passed for ministers in some Western Jewish synagogue without being at all conspicuous.)

So the two brothers were not on speaking terms.

It was my friend Franz who was the originator of this sullen silence. For George, as will soon be apparent, was of a conciliatory nature. He was the pampered darling of his mother and Franz envied him this almost more than his lame leg. He would gladly have lived in the warm proximity of his mother rather than in the arid, indifferent, alcoholic atmosphere which enveloped his father. Any praise from his father distressed him. Any caress that George might receive from his mother distressed him even more.

Franz particularly remembered holiday mealtimes in the parental household, and sometimes talked about them. There he sat, to the left of his father, opposite his mother; George sat next to his mother, opposite cousin Klara who went to a high-school in Linz and was in love with George. One might well have imagined that, in the eyes of a young girl, a crippled musician would be less important than a healthy stout-hearted cadet. But this was not so. Girls, especially those who attend high-schools with their particular emphasis on gymnastics and excursions, are captivated more by those who limp than by those who ride horses, and more by the musical than by the martial. This situation changed only during the four years of the World War, when music, gymnastics and nature, together with their male and female devotees, were drawn into the service of the Fatherland. But at the period of the silent mealtimes in Tunda's home the world was still far from war. Franz had reason enough to envy George.

It sometimes happened that they woke at the same time in the room they shared. Their eyes would meet, nothing would have been easier than for one to say 'Good morning' to the other. For so declared was their enmity that it had become almost remote, capable of being forgotten overnight – and, if not forgotten, by no means increased. But then one or other would remember – usually Franz, who would at once turn his back and go back to sleep until his brother had dressed and left the room.

XIV

After the war George married his cousin.

He married his cousin from lack of imagination, because it was convenient, because it was expected of him, out of good manners and friendly conciliation, and also for practical reasons – for she was the rich daughter of a rich landed proprietor. Only a man lacking in imagination could have married her, for she was one of those women who are labelled 'good friends', who give a man support rather than love. They can be turned to good use by anyone who happens to be a mountaineer or a cyclist or a circus acrobat or even a cripple in a wheelchair. But what a normal man is to make of them I have always failed to understand.

Klara – I find the very name revealing – was a good friend. Her hand resembled her name; it was so simple, so healthy, so trustworthy, so dependable, so honest, that it lacked only calluses; it was the hand of a gymnastics instructor. Whenever she had to greet a man, Klara feared that he might kiss her hand. So she developed the habit of giving a quite special handshake, a stout and resolute handshake which depressed a man's entire forearm – the handshake in itself was a gymnastic exercise from which one emerged invigorated. In Germany and England, in Sweden, Denmark, Norway, in many Protestant countries, there are women who clasp a man's hand in this fashion. It is a demonstration in favour of equal rights for the sexes and of hygiene, it is an important aspect of humanity's battle against germs and gallantry.

Klara's legs were matter-of-fact straight legs, legs for hiking, in no sense instruments of love – rather of sport, without calves. It seemed an indefensible luxury that they were sheathed in silk stockings. Somewhere she must have had knees – I always used to imagine that somewhere they must merge into thighs; it would hardly be possible for stockings to grow into panties just like that. But so it was, and Klara was no creature of love. True, she had something resembling a bosom, but it served only as a container for her practical goodness; whether it held a heart, who can tell?

My conscience is not very clear over this description of Klara. For it seems to me sinful to judge one of the most virtuous persons I have ever met principally on the grounds of her secondary sexual characteristics. It goes without saying that she was virtuous; what else could she be? She had a child, naturally by her own husband, the conductor – and although it is in no way a sin but, on the contrary, a virtue to have children by one's own husband, Klara's legitimate honourable pregnancy seemed like an escapade, and when she suckled the child it was like the eighth wonder, anomalous and sinful at the same time.

Moreover, the child – it was a girl – could ride a bicycle in her fourth year.

Klara had acquired and inherited her social sense from her father, the rich landed proprietor. Social sense is a luxury which the rich allow themselves and which has the further practical advantage of serving, to some extent, to maintain property. Her father loved to drink a little glass of wine with his head forester, to take a brandy with the forester, and to exchange a word with the assistant forester. Even social sense is able to make subtle distinctions. He would never allow any of his servants to pull on his boots, he used a bootjack out of common decency. His children had to wash in snow in the winter, travel the long road to school alone, climb up to their pitch-dark rooms at eight o'clock and make their own beds. Nowhere in the neighbourhood were domestic servants better treated. Klara had to iron her vests with her own hands. In short, the old man was a man of principle and fibre, a virtuous landowner, a living defence against socialism, respected far and wide and elected to the Reichstag, where he demonstrated as a member of a conservative party that reaction and humanity are not irreconcilable opposites.

He attended Klara's wedding, behaved well to the conductor, and died some weeks later without ever having allowed his expression to betray that he would have preferred a landowner : humanity to the grave.

XV

George was complaisant. There are some qualities which can only be designated by a foreign word. A complaisant man has a more difficult life than one might think; the difficulties he has to cope with can close in on him in such a way that behind his smile, he becomes a tragic figure. George, who only knew success, who was much in demand with the ladies, who directed not only the orchestra of the opera theatre but also part of the citizenry – George was unhappy. He was very much alone in the midst of a well-disposed world of personal and general goodwill. He would have preferred to live in a hostile or a neutral world. His affability did not oppress his conscience but his intellect, which was about as great as the intellect of disagreeable men with many enemies. Every lie he told choked him. He would rather have told the truth. And so, at the last moment, his tongue would upset the resolve of his brain and instead of the truth there would ring out – often to George's own surprise – some polite, rounded remark of an enigmatic, pleasant, melodious nature. Such men are often to be found by the Danube and the Rhine, the two legendary German rivers; few of the rough Nibelungs remain.

George did not love his brother; he suspected him of being the only one to see through his lies. He was glad when no more was heard of Franz. Missing! What a word! What an excuse for being sad, pleasantly sad, a new, hitherto unpractised complaisance. All the same, George was the only one who could help Franz for the time being.

Therefore I informed Herr George Tunda that his brother had returned.

Klara was overjoyed. For now her goodness, for so long undeployed and lying fallow, found a new object. Franz received two invitations, one cordially sincere and one cordially formal. The second, naturally, originated from George. Franz, however, who had not seen his brother for fifteen years and therefore had little means of knowing – although George imagined that Franz would see through him directly – Franz, who had hated his brother solely on account of the music, Franz travelled to the Rhine, to the city where they had a good opera, and some of the better reputed poets.

66

XVI

He had to change trains once on the way. He did not halt anywhere. Of Germany he saw only the stations, the sign-boards, the posters, the churches, the hotels by the railway, the silent grey streets of the suburbs, and the suburban trains looking like tired animals emerging from their stables. He saw only the changing passengers, solitary gentlemen in cutaways, carrying brief-cases, who balefully regarded every open window and occupied an empty seat with the threatening resolution of a fortress. They seemed to be waiting in readiness for an enemy who, to their chagrin, never arrived. Meanwhile they studied the papers they had extracted from their brief-cases with the zeal with which one prepares for an imminent campaign. They must have been important papers, for the gentlemen sheltered them in their arms, cradled them, as it were, under their wings, so that they might not meet with any unauthorized glance.

Other, less austere gentlemen without brief-cases, in the latest grey travelling outfits, sat themselves down with a sigh, amiably inspected those sitting opposite, and soon initiated a conversation with an earnest, moralistic, if not currently political content. Here and there a hunter climbed in, in his right hand a rifle in a brown leather case, in his left – or perhaps the other way round – a stick with an antler as handle. It seemed both genial and menacing.

Tunda thought longingly of the Russian railways and their harmless, garrulous passengers.

In every carriage there hung maps and scenic views, advertisements for German wine and cigarettes, for scenery, mountains, valleys, leather coats, dining-cars, newspapers and magazines, for chains with which to fasten one's suitcases so securely to the luggage-racks that prospective thieves would get caught up in them, too, and one could comfortably lay hold of the miscreants on returning from the dining-car and hand them over to the station-master for a reward. But one might also – if one wanted to make easy money – insure oneself against so-called journey-thefts, by which was meant not the theft of a journey but that incidental to a journey, against railway accidents, in readiness for which pickaxes, hatchets and saws were displayed warningly in glass cases. It was possible to insure one's own life, one's children and one's grandchildren, so that one raced gaily through tunnels in the expectation of an imminent collision, emerged disappointed from the gloom, and survived to eat frankfurters with mustard at the next station.

What a dependable undertaking! The magazines, the sausages, the bottles of mineral water, the cigarettes, the trunks and mailbags lay tidily on shelves, behind glass, in tinfoil and on wheeled carts; and when the train glided out of the great halls which resembled cathedrals, it seemed as if those left behind, waving handkerchiefs, crying, calling out till the very last moment, also glided away as if on roller-skates. Even the stations did not stand still. Only the signal-boxes and the signals stood like posts of honour. That they did not shoot up into the air seemed a dereliction of duty.

Tunda stood in the corridor and smoked. He did not see the notice which strictly forbade this because men do not see the irrelevant. Thus Nature wills it. In any case, another gentleman was also smoking, but he concealed his cigarette in the hollow of his hand when his practised ear heard the guard coming. The guard certainly saw the hidden cigarette but did not call this honest gentleman to account, for most authorities are concerned less with the observance of regulations than with the respect that is due to them. The guard merely drew Tunda's attention to the fact that he would incur penalties, under certain circumstances, that is if he, the guard, did not happen to be such a good-natured man. Whereupon Tunda obediently stubbed out his cigarette, unfortunately on the window pane. The honest gentleman, who seemed bent on voluntarily assuming the duties of the guard, took the opportunity to say that ashtrays were available for stubbing out cigarettes, albeit in the compartments.

Tunda, taken to task from two sides, endeavoured by civility to evade a threatening lecture, expressed his thanks, bowed his excuses, and began to praise the scenery, to some extent to get his own back. The gentleman asked if he was a foreigner. Tunda was as delighted as a schoolboy who makes a human contact with his form-master and has the privilege of carrying his exercise-books home. He readily announced that he had come straight from Siberia, by way of Vienna.

In the light of this circumstance the gentleman opined that it was natural that Tunda should have attempted to stub out his cigarette on the window pane.

Probably there were lice, too, in Siberia.

'Indeed there are lice in Siberia,' said Tunda accommodatingly.

'Where exactly?' asked the gentleman, in a high voice which emerged from a glassy larynx.

'Why, everywhere where people live,' replied Tunda.

'Surely not where clean folk live,' said the gentleman.

'There are clean folk living even in Siberia,' said Tunda.

'You seem very fond of the country?' asked the gentleman ironically.

'I love it,' Tunda acknowledged.

Thereupon ensued a pause.

The gentleman said nothing for a few minutes.

'It's easy to get used to foreign countries.'

'Under certain circumstances, yes.'

'I was in Italy last spring,' began the gentleman – 'Venice, Rome, Sicily – a belated honeymoon, you understand, there was never any time while I was studying – excuse me – '

Here the gentleman underwent a remarkable transformation, he was suddenly a head taller, his bleary eyes flashed bold and blue, a tiny co-ordinate system of creases appeared over the bridge of his nose.

'Excuse me,' said the gentleman, bowing stiffly: 'Public Prosecutor Brandsen.'

At the same time he clicked his heels together with a sharp crack.

For a moment Tunda believed himself in danger of imminent arrest.

He collected himself, became equally serious, made a noise with his boots, assumed an alert posture, and rattled off his name:

'First Lieutenant Tunda.'

After the Public Prosecutor had inspected him for a space of time, he resumed the narrative of his postponed honeymoon.

A later development was that the State Prosecutor actually offered Tunda a cigarette, surreptitiously glanced right and left for the guard, and declared with respect to him:

'A fine fellow!'

'A conscientious man!' added Tunda.

This designation seemed to irritate the Public Prosecutor; perhaps he did not take kindly to the conjunction of 'conscientious' and 'man'. He therefore said only:

'Come, come!'

So passing the time, they arrived at the city on the Rhine.

XVII

It was ten at night.

On the platform stood men with umbrellas, their clothes damp. The arc-lights swayed and cast faint shadows on the damp stones. A great many gnats settled on the arc-lights and were rocked to and fro. They attracted attention because they noticeably dimmed the light emitted without, however, obscuring the fact that they *were* arc-lights.

Everyone was disconcerted by the poor illumination the lamps supplied, looked up and shook their heads at the insects' insolence.

Tunda, a heavy bag in his hand, looked around for a familiar face.

Naturally, Klara had come to meet him. George had stayed at home for various reasons. In the first place, it was a Saturday night, when the Club met. This club was a meeting-place for the academicians of the Rhenish city, artists and journalists, and only those of other voca-

tions who possessed an honorary doctorate. The city itself had a university which distributed honorary doctorates like admission cards to the Club, for it was not
possible to revoke the rules which permitted only academicians to be enrolled. The pressure on the Club and
on the honorary doctorates had gradually mounted to
the extent that the University had had to institute a
numerus clausus for benefactors from industrial circles,
while another *numerus clausus* for foreign Jews had
already existed for a number of years. This *numerus
clausus* against foreign Jews had been carried by the
native Jews, who maintained that their ancestors had
deliberately travelled with the Romans to the Rhine
before the time of the great migrations. The Jews almost
appeared to be saying that their ancestors had allowed
the Teutons themselves to settle by the Rhine, wherefore
it was the grateful duty of the modern Germans to
protect these Rhenish-Roman Jews from the Polish
ones.

George was at this club today.

In the second place, he did not come to the station
because he would thereby have deprived Klara of her
old-established privilege of dealing on her own with all
those affairs which, in other families, usually require a
masculine hand.

In the third place, George did not come because he
was a little nervous of his brother and because a peaceable brother, once he was in his room and possibly even
in bed, was much less dangerous than one just getting
off the train.

Klara was wearing a leather jerkin of brown calf,
reminiscent of the leather shirts worn beneath their
armour by the knights of the Middle Ages. She gave the
impression that she had come from afar, had faced

perils in gloomy forests, she conjured up civil war. She came up to Tunda with the frank and resonant cordiality of awkward upright persons.

'I recognized you immediately,' she said.

Then she kissed him on the mouth. She attempted to relieve him of his heavy bag. He could not wrest it away from her and ran beside her like a child collected from school by a maid-servant.

In front of the station he saw a maze of wires, arc-lights, automobiles; in the middle a policeman who extended his arms like an automaton – right, left, upward, downward – simultaneously signalling on a whistle and giving the impression that the very next moment he would have to use his legs, too, to regulate the traffic. Tunda admired him. Music issued from various taverns, filling the intervals occasionally left by the din of the traffic; the atmosphere was one of Sunday enjoyment, clinking of glasses, coal, industry, the big city and general well-being.

The station appeared to be a centre of civilization.

By the time Tunda had regained his senses, they had already stopped in front of the conductor's villa.

A grille began to rumble as soon as a knob was pressed and at once glided smoothly open. A servant stood there in a blue livery and bowed like a nobleman. They walked over crunching wet gravel, it felt like sand between the teeth. Then came a few steps, at the top of which, under a silver lantern, stood a girl in white like an angel, with wings at the back of her head, soft brown eyes and knees that curtseyed. Then they entered a brown-panelled hall in which one looked in vain for antlers, but found a mask of Beethoven standing in for hunting-gear.

For the master of this house was a conductor.

'You must be rich!' said Tunda, who sometimes reverted to his former naïvety.

'Not rich!' smiled Klara deprecatingly, her social conscience outraged more by the word than the fact.

'It's just that we live in a civilized fashion. It's essential for George.'

George did not come home for an hour.

He was wearing a dinner-jacket, his cheeks were flushed and smoothly powdered, he smelled of wine and shaving-soap, which produced the effect of menthol.

Franz and George embraced for the first time in their lives.

Some years previously the conductor had bought a silver samovar from some Russian refugees, as a curiosity. In honour of his brother, who must have become a kind of Russian, this item of furniture was brought in on a trolley by the liveried servant. The servant wore white gloves and seized small pieces of charcoal with silver sugar-tongs to heat the samovar.

A stench as from a light railway locomotive arose.

At this juncture Franz had to explain how to manage a samovar. He had never used one in Russia, did not understand it, but relied on his intuition.

Meanwhile he noticed many Jewish appurtenances in the room – lamps, goblets, scrolls of the Torah.

'Have you been converted to Judaism?' he asked.

It emerged that in this city, where the oldest and most impoverished Jewish families dwelled, many costly artefacts of artistic value were to be had for a song. In addition, other rooms contained Buddhas, although no Buddhists lived anywhere near the Rhine; there were also Hussite manuscripts, a Lutheran bible, Catholic religious furniture, ebony madonnas and Russian ikons.

That's how conductors live.

Franz Tunda slept in a room devoted to modern painting. But Thomas Mann's *The Magic Mountain* lay on his bedside table.

XVIII

When he awoke next day, it was Sunday.

Ultra-modern bells, fashioned out of war material by gun-factories converted to peaceful purposes, called the world to prayer.

The house smelled of coffee. At breakfast Tunda was informed that it was caffeine-free coffee, which did not harm the heart and pleased the palate.

The conductor was still asleep. Artists need sleep. Klara, however, even in her married state, had not forgotten the healthy usages of her parental home. She awoke like a bird with the first rays of the sun. Wearing thin rubber gloves such as surgeons use she wiped the dust from the religious objects.

Tunda decided to go for a stroll.

He went in the direction from which came the occasional sound of tramcar bells. He walked along quiet streets with gardens in which well-dressed boys and girls on bicycles wove harmonious loops. Servant-girls returned from divine service to flirt. Dogs lay haughtily behind the grilles like lions. Closed venetian blinds evoked the holidays.

Then Tunda came upon the old quarter of the town, with its coloured gables and wine-cellars with Middle High German names. Shabbily-dressed men came towards him, evidently workers who lived among these

Gothic characters but probably earned their living in the pits of international owners.

Music sounded. Young men armed with sticks, marched behind fifes and drums in double-column. It sounded like the music of ghosts or some militarized Aeolian harps. The young folk marched with serious faces and without saying a word; they marched towards an ideal.

Behind and beside them, on the pavements and in the middle of the road, men and women kept in step; it was their way of taking a walk.

All were marching towards the station, which looked like a temple. Porters squatted on the stone steps like numbered beggars; the engines whistled with holiness and reverence.

The double columns fell out and disappeared into the station.

At this point the supporters turned back, slackening their pace, their faces transfigured, the echo of the whistles still in their hearts. As if they had fulfilled a joyous duty, they could now devote themselves to Sunday with a clear conscience.

Along the streets scuttled painted prostitutes, off duty. They conjured up thoughts of death. Some wore glasses.

A group of cyclists sped by ringing their bells. Men with dignified bearing and childish clothing, carrying rucksacks, hiked off to the mountains.

Odd, scattered, gleaming firemen strolled with wives and children.

The attractions of grand, double-bill military concerts were announced on bill-boards by district ex-servicemen's associations.

Behind the great plate-glass windows of the cafés whipped cream towered before epicures in wicker chairs.

A comically misshapen dwarf sold shoe-laces.

An epileptic lay twitching in the sun. A crowd of people stood around him. One man expounded the case as if he was giving a lecture to students; the thesis of his exposition was that the man should always stay in the shade.

Young men passed by in small groups with caps that were much too small, black-wrapped faces and glassy eyes behind glassy spectacles. These were students.

In the distance roared the Rhine.

Then other men arrived, with students' caps made out of paper.

These were not students but chimney-sweeps, washed clean, who had organized some festivity.

Elderly gentlemen took dogs, and elderly ladies, for walks.

Verdigrised church steeples rose up in the distance. Singing rang out from the wine-cellars.

Shadows suddenly grew dense over the city, a brisk downpour descended, women in white revealed their frilly petticoats like a second summer of linen.

Black umbrellas were hoisted over shining bright clothes. It all resembled a dreamlike, somewhat precipitate, wet funeral.

Tunda became hungry, forgot that he had no money, and entered a wine-cellar. When he saw the prices on the menu he decided to turn back, but three waiters barred his way.

'I've no money!' said Tunda.

'Just tell us your name,' said a waiter.

When he did give his name, Tunda was treated as if it were he who was the conductor.

He began to be impressed by his brother.

A hunchback entered the establishment, wretched

77

and ill; with imploring eyes and timorous shaky legs he slunk from table to table, laying a handbill on each.

On the handbill Tunda read:

> Dance and gymnastics.
> Physical training: relaxation and muscular exercise.
> Elasticity, vaulting, impulse, walking, running.
> Jumping, eurhythmics, spatial perception,
>   choreography.
> Harmonious movement, eternal youth.
> Group improvisation to musical accompaniment.

He ate, drank and went out.

The street now seemed unfamiliar. The wet stones had dried quickly. There was a rainbow in the sky. The trams went ponderously by, packed with people seeking nature's embrace. Drunks tripped over themselves. The cinemas opened their doors. The commissionaires, in gold-rimmed caps, stood shouting and distributing handbills to the passers-by. The sun lay on the upper stories of the houses.

Wizened old women walked through the streets in cloth bonnets trimmed with tinkling glass cherries. The women looked as if they had emerged from old chests-of-drawers which Sunday had opened wide. When they stepped into the wide squares in the late sun, they cast oddly long shadows; there were so many of them that they resembled a procession of legendary old witches.

The clouds that passed across the sky were made of mother-of-pearl, like shirt-studs. They stood in an enigmatic but clearly perceptible relationship to the thick amber cigarette-holders which a large number of men held between their lips.

The sunlight became more and more intermittent,

the mother-of-pearl more pallid. People were crowding back from the sports-grounds, bringing sweat in their train and releasing dust. Motor-horns moaned like run-over dogs.

Prostitutes appeared in dark doorways, pulled along by St Bernards and poodles. Spectral caretakers, glued to their chairs, glided out of doors to savour the Sunday evening.

Young working-class girls shrieked, workers walked in their Sunday-best, with green hats, in lopsided suits, their hands feeling heavy and superfluous.

Soldiers passed like walking advertisements. The scent of dead flowers recalled All Souls' Day.

High above the streets arc-lights swayed precariously, like storm-lanterns. Balls of paper swirled in dusty parks. A hesitant wind arose, gust after gust.

It was as if the town were quite uninhabited, as if – on Sundays only – the dead came on leave from the cemeteries.

One imagined yawning waiting tombs.

When it was evening Tunda went home.

The conductor was giving a small celebration in his honour.

XIX

It was a small Sunday party, although the guests did not give the impression that they needed to wait for Sunday to participate in such a gathering. For they belonged to the elevated ranks, those ranks which could also be invited on Wednesdays, or Thursdays, or even Mondays, and were so invited. They included artists, academics and councillors. A deputy mayor who had musical interests was among the guests; also a professor from the University, who gave readings on Friday evenings between six and eight and was frequented by society ladies; an actor who had played successfully at the Staatstheater in Berlin; a petite young actress who had undoubtedly slept with the stout deputy mayor, but had re-emerged from his embrace unharmed and even, to some extent, invigorated; a museum director who had written about some of van Gogh's works, though his heart lay with Böcklin; the music critic of one of the larger newspapers, who seemed to have concluded an implicit pact with the conductor.

One or two of them had brought their wives. These ladies fell into two categories : the elegant, who exhibited Parisian leanings; and the prosaic, who reminded one of the Masurian lakes. The latter were burnished with a glitter of steel and victory. Three groups formed: first, the prosaic ladies; second, the elegant ladies; and third, the men. Only Franz and his sister-in-law oscillated between the three groups, dispensing refreshments. Around Franz, decked in his Siberian halo and exhaling the great breath of the steppes and the polar sea, competed the bold glances of a number of the elegant women. Men clapped him on the back and told him what it was like in Siberia. The music critic enquired about the new music in Russia. But he did not wait for an answer and began a discourse on the conductorless Moscow Orchestra. The museum director knew the Hermitage in St Petersburg inside out. The professor, who despised Marx, quoted the places in which Lenin contradicted himself. He was even familiar with Trotsky's book about the genesis of the Red Army.

There was no particular structure to the conversation. To bring this about, a manufacturer was called on who only arrived around midnight. He had an honorary doctorate and was a member of the Club. Red-faced, with the desperately clutching hands of a drowning man, even though he was standing with both feet on solid ground, he began to cross-examine Tunda.

The manfacturer had concessions in Russia. 'What is the state of the industries in the Urals?' he asked.

'I don't know,' Tunda confessed.

'And what about the petroleum in Baku?'

'Quite good,' said Tunda, feeling that he had lost ground.

'Are the workers contented?'

'Not always!'

'Exactly,' said the manufacturer. 'So the workers are not satisfied. But you know damn-all about Russia, my dear friend. One loses one's perspective about things when one is close to them, I know. It's nothing to be ashamed of, dear friend.'

'Yes,' said Tunda, 'one loses perspective. One is so close to things that they cease to be of concern. Just as you give no thought to how many buttons there are on your waistcoat. One can live in the present as if deep in a forest. One encounters people and sheds them again as trees shed leaves. Can't you understand that it doesn't seem to me to be of the slightest importance how much petroleum they extract in Baku? It's a marvellous city. When a wind springs up in Baku . . .'

'You are a poet,' said the manufacturer.

'Do they read Ilya Ehrenburg in Russia?' asked the little actress. 'He is a sceptic.'

'I've never heard that name; who is he?' said the professor severely.

'He is a young Russian author,' said Frau Klara, to the general astonishment.

'Are you going to Paris this year?' one of the Parisian group of women asked another.

'I've been looking at the latest hats in *Femina*, pot-shaped again, and the costume jackets are slightly belled out. I don't think it's worth the trouble this year.'

'My husband and I were in Berlin last week,' said the music critic's wife. 'There's a city that's growing at a tremendous rate. The women get more elegant every day.'

'Fantastic, fantastic,' opined the manufacturer. 'That city leaves the rest of Germany speechless.'

He introduced some story on the theme of Berlin. He always knew exactly when to provide a new focus for the flagging conversation.

He talked about industry and of the new Germany, the workers and the decline of Marxism, politics and the League of Nations, art and Max Reinhardt.

The manufacturer betook himself to an adjoining room. He lay down, half-hidden by a copper font, a Catholic rarity, on a broad sofa. He had loosened his patent-leather shoes, undone his collar, his shirt-front gaped like a double folding door, a silk handkerchief lay on his bare chest. That was how Tunda found him.

'I understood you perfectly well earlier, Herr Tunda,' said the manufacturer. 'I understood perfectly what you meant about the wind in Baku. I understood perfectly that you have experienced a great deal, and that we come along in our ignorance and ask you stupid questions. As far as I'm concerned, I put my practical questions for purely selfish reasons. It was, to some extent, my duty. You won't understand that just yet. You'll have to live with us a little longer first. Then you too

82

will have to pose specific questions and give specific answers. Everyone here lives by established rules and against his will. Naturally, in the beginning, that is when he first came here, we each had our own opinion. We arranged our lives perfectly freely, no one interfered with us. But after a time, almost without our noticing it, what we had arranged out of free choice became, without actually being written down, a divine decree and so ceased to be the consequence of our choice. All our later thoughts and actions had to be forced through against this decree. Or else we had to circumvent it in some way; we had, so to speak, to wait until it closed its eyes for a moment, out of fatigue. But you are not yet acquainted with this decree.

'You haven't as yet any idea what terribly wide-open eyes it has, eyelids stuck to its brows which never close. For instance, when I first came here, I liked wearing coloured shirts with attached collars and without cuffs; but, as time passed it was really in obedience to a very powerful and immutable decree that I *should* wear this kind of shirt. You cannot imagine how difficult it was for practical reasons – for this was a period when things were going badly for me – to wear white shirts with detachable collars. The decree ordained : manufacturer X wears coloured shirts with attached collars, thereby establishing that he is one of the working people, like his workers and employees. He need only undo his tie, and at once he appears a proletarian. Then, gradually and quite circumspectly, as if I had stolen them from someone, I began to wear white shirts. First once a week, for on that day the decree deigns occasionally to turn a blind eye, then on Saturday afternoons, then on Fridays. When I wore a white shirt for the first time on a Wednesday – Wednesday is my unlucky day anyway – everyone, including my secretary at the office and my foreman in the factory, looked at me reproachfully.

'Now shirts may not be very important. But they are symbolic. At least, in this case. And it is the same with the really important things. If I came here as a manufacturer, do you think I could ever become a conductor, even if I were ten times better than your brother? Or do you think that your brother could ever become a manufacturer? Now, for all I care, vocation is not such an important matter. It's not so important how one makes one's living. But what is important, for example, is love for one's wife and child. Once you elect voluntarily to be a good paterfamilias, do you think you can ever stop? If, one day, you have announced to your cook: "I don't like white meat," do you think you can change your mind ten years later? When I first came here I was very busy, I had to make money, organize a factory – for you must know that I am the son of a Jewish pedlar – I had no time for the theatre, art, music, crafts, religious objects, the Jewish community or Catholic cathedral. So if anyone got too close to me in any connection, I repelled him in a boorish manner. I was, so to say, a boor or a man of action, people were amazed at my energy. The decree seized hold of me, ordained my boorishness, my uncouth behaviour – you will understand that I am compelled to speak to you as the decree lays down. Who ordered me to take up concessions in this stinking Russia? The decree! Don't you think the wind in Baku interests me more than petroleum? But dare I ask you about the wind? Am I a meteorologist? What would the decree have to say about it?

'And everyone lies, just as I do. Everyone says what the decree prescribes. The little actress who was asking you earlier about a Russian writer is probably more interested in petroleum. But no, the roles are all allotted. The music critic and your brother, for instance. I know they both gamble on the stock exchange. But what do they talk about? About cultural matters. When you enter a room and see other people present, you know at once what each has to say. Each has his role. That's how it is in our city. The skin in which each one hides is not his own. And just as it is in our city, so it is everywhere, in at least a hundred great cities in our country.

'Look, I was in Paris. Let's forget the fact that, after my return, I dared tell no one that I would rather live as a poor man in Paris under a Seine bridge than in our city with an average-sized factory. No one would believe me, I even doubt myself whether it is what I really wanted. But there's something else I want to tell you. Someone accosts me in the Avenue de l'Opéra. He wants to show me the brothels. Naturally I am cautious; the man seeks to dispel my scruples. He enumerates his clients. He mentions the name of the very Minister with whom I had been negotiating the previous week. He not only names names, he has proof. He shows me letters. Yes, it is the Minister's handwriting. "Dear Davidowiczi," writes the Minister, obviously a good friend of Davidowiczi. Why does he call him "Dear"? Because the Minister has a very peculiar perversion. Because day and night he things only of goats, and nothing else. I ask you, goats! And he is not even the Minister of Agriculture! He sets about the negotiations with unbelievable zeal. One feels sure that his department can rely on him. And on what are his thoughts fixed? On animals. Who forbids him to speak of what really concerns him? The decree.'

The manufacturer had hurriedly to rearrange his clothing because of the approach of two ladies. Strange to relate, it was one of the prosaic group with one of the

Parisian group. They were discussing clothes; it looked as if the prosaic lady was seeking information from the elegant one.

'He need not,' whispered the manufacturer, 'have spoken as freely about animals to Davidowiczi as he did. He could have referred to them in a roundabout way, for instance to their usefulness in domestic economy. But he did not even do that. Who does? How many things do you think would be uncovered if we could rummage in the closets of each individual – and, more than that, in their innermost secret recesses?

'When you spoke of the wind, tears came to my eyes. But do you think I would have dared to weep? I dared only bluster.

'I confess to you that I sometimes go to the cinema just to have a good cry. Yes, the cinema.'

A lady approached, saw Tunda and smiled at him in a gracious, enticing yet aloof manner, as if she held a tape measure in front of her body, as if there were a specific law which laid down that only a certain number of teeth should be exposed when smiling.

'And were you never homesick?' she enquired. 'We used to speak of you occasionally. Because you were missing.' She inclined her head as she mentioned the word. She found it embarrassing to have to say to a man's face that he had been missing. It was a painful, possibly even an improper condition to be missing. It was something like telling a living person that he has been taken for dead.

'Your brother has often told us about you. How you were both in love with your cousin Klara when you came home for Christmas and Easter, and how you almost got angry with each other on that account. And how you said goodbye when you went off to the war (she very nearly said 'marched') and kissed your brother who was so grieved that he was compelled to stay at home on account of his leg. Yes, we often spoke of you. Did you sometime think that people might be talking about you, as if . . .'

She did not finish the sentence. Possibly she had intended to say: 'As if you were dead.' But one does not say that to the face of the living.

Franz was astonished by these stories his brother had told.

In any case, the only thing to say to a woman who talks about such things is 'Let's sit down!' So they sat down. The conductor's house offered many facilities for sitting down; and it was a particular quality of these facilities that one no sooner sat down than one lay back, a usage which seemed to be linked with feminine fashions. The clothes that were worn called for recumbency or, at any rate, they called recumbency to mind. Moreover, a certain renunciation of European customs was evident.

So Tunda sat down with the lady behind the broad brown back of a Buddha, almost as in an arbour, behind wild vines. The lady's smoothly shaved legs lay side by side like two similarly clad sisters, both in silk sheaths. Tunda laid a hand on one leg, but the lady seemed quite unaware of it. Whenever steps approached she endeavoured to draw away.

Ah, what will one not do for a missing person?

If Tunda had exploited to the full the possibilities afforded by his Siberian glamour and by the solid city of the religious setting, his fate might possibly have been postponed but in no way averted. Whether he turned them to advantage later I do not know.

XX

After the guests had departed, the brothers remained alone in one of the rooms; alone, if one takes no account of pictures, gods and saints. Tunda was unaccustomed to these silent witnesses; and, for my part, I have no use for lackeys who stand behind my chair counting the hairs on my head. There would certainly have been lackeys in the conductor's house, had it not been for Frau Klara's social conscience. It was manifestly repugnant to her to degrade men so.

However, this was not the case with the gods.

Furthermore, there was in the room where they sat, installed by Frau Klara, one of those practical inventions which has been called the housewife's delight.

It was a remarkable lamp, a soft standard lamp whose light emerged through numerous small apertures of equal circumference perforating its fragile transparent body. But the object of this lamp was not so much to illuminate as to devour the smoke which had collected in the room during the course of the evening. This lamp obviated the need for open windows, draughts, chills — and ultimately the doctor. Excellent inventions of this kind are made in Germany and America every year. The conductor, too, was making use of one; that is, he smoked nicotine-free cigarettes. And even their smoke was gobbled up by the magic lamp.

It was a hygienic home without parallel.

'Good night!' said Klara, after she had installed the lamp, coming over to give her husband a hearty kiss on the forehead. It was a sex-free kiss, devoid of eroticism. Franz received a similar one, but nevertheless found himself somewhat aroused. He pushed back his chair and endeavoured to stand up, but his sister-in-law pressed him down by his shoulders.

So now the two brothers were left alone and had to converse for the first time.

The conductor, who was well-known for his skill in glossing over difficult overtures, was the first to utter and sensibly chose a neutral topic:

'How does our town strike you?'

Nothing is so contagious as polite sociability. Franz suppressed the most important and major part of his opinion and replied:

'I had pictured it as gayer, more lively, more Rhenish in fact.'

'It has a pleasant and peaceable population. The working class is not so radicalized here as elsewhere. The Lord Mayor is a member of the German People's Party, the Burgomaster and his deputy are Social Democrats. The are even five members of the Social Democratic Party in my orchestra. The bass-player is very good, in fact.'

'What's so surprising about that?' asked Franz. 'Why should the Party prevent anyone from being a good bass-player?'

'Certainly!' said the conductor. 'Political activity is unfavourable to art. Art is something sacred, something separate from daily life. Whoever serves it practises an almost priestly vocation. Can you conceive of anyone delivering a political speech and then conducting Parsifal?'

'I can conceive,' said Franz, 'that under certain circumstances a political speech may be just as important as Parsifal. A good politician can be as important as a good musician. A priest he certainly is not. A concert-hall is no more a temple of art than a meeting-house is a temple of politics.'

'You have lost your European outlook,' said the conductor softly and soothingly, like a nerve specialist. 'Unfortunately, similar views have already affected a large part of Germany. They emanate from Berlin. But here, on the Rhine, there are still a few old bastions of the established bourgeois culture. Our traditions extend from antiquity through the Middle Ages, the Humanistic period, the Renaissance, German Romanticism . . .'

'Is this European culture?' asked Franz, pointing to the Buddhas, the cushions, the deep wide sofas, the oriental carpets.

'It seems to me that you've borrowed from other sources as well. Tonight, your guests danced some negro dances which are probably not to be found in Parsifal. I can't understand how you can still speak of German culture. Where is it? In the way the women dress? The manufacturer you had here today, has he got European culture? As a matter of fact, I liked him better than the others because he despises all of you. This ancient culture of yours has developed a thousand holes. You plug the holes by borrowing from Asia, Africa, America. But, the holes go on growing. You retain the European uniform, the dinner-jacket and pale complexion, but you dwell in mosques and Indian temples. If I were you, I should wear a burnous.'

'We make a few concessions,' said the conductor, 'nothing more. The world has grown smaller; Africa, Asia and America are nearer to us. Foreign customs have been adopted in all ages and become a part of culture.'

'But where is the culture of which you would have

them become a part? You have only the trappings of an ancient culture. Are the students with their ill-fitting coloured caps ancient German culture? Or your station, whose greatest miracle is that trains arrive there and depart again? Are you looking for culture in your wine-cellars, where they sing "A Rhenish Maiden" when they're tight and dance the Charleston when they're sober? Or do you find ancient culture in the cosy gabled roofs that house your workers – not artisans or goldsmiths or watch-makers, not master-singers but pro-letarians, who live in the pits and are at home in electric lifts but not among your unreadable Gothic script? That's just a masquerade, not reality! You never get out of your fancy-dress! Today I saw a fireman in his glittering uniform pushing a pram. There was no fire anywhere, all was peaceful. Was it a children's nurse who had dressed up as a fireman, or a fireman who wanted to play at being a children's nurse? There were students wearing cloth caps and townsfolk wearing students' paper caps. Was it the students or the towns-folk who were in disguise? Then I saw a few young people in velvet caps, with sailors' trousers; I asked a waiter, who informed me that this was an old form of carpenters' dress. Is that correct? Do they make coffins and cradles with velvet caps on their heads? Do people still roam the high-roads with bundles when there are hardly any high-roads left, only motor-cars and aero-planes?'

'You've seen a lot in one day,' said the complaisant conductor. 'I never walk in the streets.'

'Why not? Doesn't it interest you? Because you're a high priest of art, doesn't it suit you to mingle with the people? Are you satisfied among your fonts and pictures and among your ancient culture? Do you learn everything from the newspapers?'

'I don't read any newspapers!' smiled the conductor. 'I only read about musical matters.'

'Why, even in the Cadet School I knew more about the world than you!' said Franz. 'We've never spoken to each other the whole of our lives, and now we've nothing better to do than to discuss politics as if we had met in a railway carriage.'

'So you didn't even travel by sleeping-car?' exclaimed the conductor, deeply moved.

It soon became evident that, once they had passed beyond generalities, they had nothing to say to each other.

Nothing occurred even to the complaisant conductor. Finally he decided to ask:

'Have you any news of Irene?'

'She must have got married,' said Franz.

'I've heard she lives in Paris,' said George.

Then they went to bed.

XXI

From time to time the conductor visited some larger or smaller nearby town on the Rhine, stayed away for a few days, and returned pale and in need of recuperation.

'Poor George, he has to have a change of air,' said Klara.

'I need relaxation,' said the conductor.

His excursions, as soon emerged, were for amorous purposes. He was like a bird which hops from branch to branch, and pours forth a little song from each. The young girls in the ancient centres of culture venerate the high-priests of art, together with boxers and gymnasts. In this they differ from their sisters in the larger cities, where barbarism is indigenous.

The conductor's marriage resembled a still lake over which blew a constant cool breeze. The child swam merrily between father and mother, as if between two harbours. She was never ill, she never even had whooping-cough. She did not cry. She was not moody. She had imbibed her mother's placid unintoxicating milk and formed her character correspondingly. She was the very model of a little girl. She played with dolls made from sponges with which she could be washed at the same time. She said Papa and Mama and referred to all adults as aunt and uncle with an equal friendliness.

In the conductor's house one ate a lot of vegetables and eggs, cream and fruit, and many desserts that tasted of paper. One drank wholesome table-wines and rose from table as light as an air-balloon. All the same, the conductor slept after meals, he lay down on his sofa, yet it seemed as if he was not asleep but had merely withdrawn to be alone with his private culture.

One made and received a few calls.

Within the town, itself a cultural centre, there were also houses which were smaller cultural centres. There were artists who lived in studios and played the bohemian. There was a lawyer who invited Christian fellow-citizens for the Jewish festivals, and so established an oecumenical atmosphere, at least in the higher spheres. There was a Christian designer who made his living out of Jewish ornamentation and traced the family trees of all the old Rhenish families for the appropriate fee. There was a stamp-collector who, every few weeks, organized exhibitions of his best specimens together with festivities which, now and then, resulted in a marriage. There were descendants of the old poets of the second Romantic school, who had interesting unpublished letters to show. There was a live lyric poet of repute who lived in a small room in a museum, and an old professor who sat all day in a church tower and operated the famous carillon which is mentioned in Baedeker. There was an old churchyard where the students from the Art School would spend entire mornings in order to portray the picturesque gravestones in their sketchbooks. There were a few historic old fountains which the municipality had collected one day and brought together as a single group in the city park, because it was convenient and because there was already a war-memorial there erected in 1920 and a Bismarck oak, dating from 1872 and surrounded by barbed wire, which rustled throughout the summer. There were also many owners of bicycles, which were known as the little man's motor-car.

In the end, the esteem enjoyed by the conductor extended itself to Franz, who was occasionally called on to recount his Siberian experience. To the fifty quarto pages he added a further thirty. He had already invented a miscellany of adventures; it was a simple matter for him to become a renowned Siberian expert.

My utter indolence does not distress me in the least in this town [he wrote in his journal]. If I were to work even less here, I would still consider myself very useful. There are no working people among the people I come across, with the possible exception of the manufacturers. Not even the businessmen work. It seems to me that the men still have their feet on the ground, the whole of their lower portion is of the earth, but from their hands upwards they no longer

94

live in an earthly atmosphere. Each exists of two halves. In each case the upper half is ashamed of the lower. Each considers his hands as better than his feet. Each leads two lives. Eating, drinking and loving is carried out by the lower, the inferior, parts, professional life by the upper.

When George conducts, he is a different George from the one who sleeps with his little devotees. Yesterday a lady informed me that she had been to the cinema, and had almost decided to keep her face veiled. She went to the cinema only with the lower, inferior part of her body, she watched the film only with a pair of vulgar eyes suited to vulgar purposes, eyes which were at her disposal like an opera-glass or a lorgnette. I slept with a woman who woke me after an hour in order to ask me if my spiritual love for her corresponded to my physical performance. For without the spiritual side she considered herself 'degraded'. I found that I had to get dressed very quickly, and while I was searching for my collar-stud, which had rolled under the bed, I explained to her that my soul always resided in that part of my body which I was using to carry out a particular activity. Thus, in my feet when I went for a walk, and so on.

'You are a cynic,' said the woman.

I felt much better among my stupidest comrades at the Cadet School and later in the regiment. The female auxiliaries, second class, at the base were more sensible than these ladies. The only concession they make to reality is their gymnastic exercises every morning at six o'clock. Only the gymnastics are not called gymnastics, but eurhythmics. Otherwise they would consider themselves degraded at every knees-bend.

My sister-in-law reminds me of Natasha. I would never have fallen in love with Natasha if I had taken the opposite road, from my brother's house to Russia. Natasha sacrificed to the revolutionary idea, Klara sacrifices partly to culture, partly to the social conscience. But whereas Natasha obviously behaved against her nature, Klara does not have to force herself at all. Nothing comes to her more naturally than this social conscience, which causes her to care for the health of her servants, to treat waiters like war comrades and myself as if we had sucked at the same breast. I sometimes think that she is a creature under a spell, that she might be turned in a healthy direction, that one might make a woman of her. But that is as improbable as a love affair with a vacuum-cleaner, which they push over the carpets every morning in this country.

My brother probably denies my moral justification for living. I have no vocation and earn no money. I even consider myself guilty because I eat his bread and butter. Anyway, I am quite unfitted to hold down a job anywhere unless they were to pay me for getting angry at the world. I am not even in harmony with any of the ruling ideologies.

Some days ago I got to know a woman, a writer and a communist. She has married a Rumanian communist, also a writer, whom I find untalented and stupid but who is crafty enough to conceal his stupidity in his communist convictions and to justify his laziness on political grounds. This couple lives on the support of a capitalist uncle, a banker, and by writing articles for radical magazines. The young woman wears low-heeled shoes and sneers at the society that provides her with a living. She talks to her own daughter like the warden of a reformatory to an inmate who is still a minor, regards her as an ill-tempered offshoot of the family and condones her bad behaviour. She wears an infinitely superior expression, associates with some literary people, is acquainted with a Berlin night-club, and once lived in a working-class district, out of protest and from conviction. After three months her uncle sent her money and she moved to the West. Since then she has become acquainted with the heights and depths of society and has written novels of working-class life. If one addresses her as Madam, one suffers her scorn, and if one calls her Frau Tedescu, she is shocked. She despised me from the outset because I did not remain in Russia. Naturally she is not aware that I fought in the civil war, and would probably never have believed me capable of doing so. Courtesy she considers a bourgeois vulgarity. I have discovered a special way of dealing with her. I firmly clasp her delicate little hand, shake it, call her comrade and talk bluntly of the sexual matters which she discusses in her novels. At times she is near to tears.

The only times when I become tender and melancholy are when I think of Irene. She is not even the Irene, my betrothed, whom I knew when I was still a stupid first lieutenant and her fiancé. It is some unknown woman I love, who lives I know not where.

When George told me he had heard that she was in Paris, I felt hot and cold, I was dazzled, it was like that time in Baku when the lady told me of the ridiculous shop windows of the Rue de la Paix. It is as if I had been seeking Irene all my life and every now and again someone told me he had come across her.

But in reality I don't seek her at all. I don't even yearn for her. Perhaps she really is something quite different from the rest of the world; and thinking of her is the least residue of my credulity. It's probably necessary to be a writer to express this accurately.

From time to time I feel that it is necessary for me to seek her out. If I went to Paris I would perhaps run into her. That would take money. But I can't accept anything from George. That is a ridiculous inhibition. He would probably give it me and rejoice into the bargain that I was leaving him. But, though I may take George's money for other reasons, I won't for this one.

And it's about time that I earned something. In this kind of world it is not important for me to work, but it *is* necessary for me to have an income. A man without an income is like a man without a name or like a shadow minus its body. One feels like a phantom. This does not contradict what I have written above. I have no pangs of conscience as regards my indolence, it is just that my indolence brings in no money whereas the indolence of everyone else is well remunerated. Only money confers the right to live.

XXII

At that time I was living in Berlin. One day M. said to me: 'I ran into Irene Hartmann. I greeted her. But she did not recognize me. I turned back, thinking I might have made a mistake, and greeted her again. But she did not recognize me.'

'You're sure you weren't mistaken?'

'Yes!' said M.

I thereupon wrote to Franz Tunda.

'Dear friend,' I wrote, 'I am not sure that I understand the reasons for your return. Perhaps you don't know yourself. But if it is because you want to find Irene, Herr M. came across her in Berlin recently.'

Tunda arrived a few days later.

I liked him enormously.

It takes a long time for men to acquire their particular countenances. It is as if they were born without their faces, their foreheads, their noses or their eyes. They acquire all these with the passage of time, and one must be patient; it takes time before everything is properly assembled. Tunda had only now achieved his countenance. His right eyebrow was higher than the left. This gave him an expression of permanent surprise, of a man arrogantly astonished at the singular circumstances of this world; he had the face of a very aristocratic man compelled to sit at table with ill-mannered persons and observing their conduct with condescending, patient but in no way indulgent curiosity. His glance was at once shrewd and tolerant. He had the look of a man who puts up with much suffering in order to gain experience. He seemed so sagacious that one might almost take him for benevolent. But, in reality, he seemed to me already to possess that degree of sagacity that makes a man truly indifferent.

'Then you want to see Irene?'

' Yes,' he said. 'When I got your letter I wanted to see her. Now I feel less certain about it again. Maybe it would be enough just to look at her and then go away satisfied.'

'Let's assume that you do meet up with her. She is

happily married, probably loves her husband with the kind of love which is composed of habit, gratitude, shared experiences – the physical experience that results from many hours of intimacy – occasional eruptions of passion, the familiarity that no longer has a place for modesty. Do you believe that she would fling her arms around your neck simply out of the grateful recollection of an engagement which didn't come off? Do you love her with the passion to which she would be entitled? Above all, would it be what you really want?'

'These are things,' said Tunda, 'which have to happen before I can tell whether there is any basis for them. If I had gone straight home to Irene, my life would have taken another turn. A chain of circumstances prevented me from doing so. I will admit to you that I reproach myself. I reproach myself for having submitted to circumstances without putting up a fight. I now feel that I must seek out Irene in order to rehabilitate myself. The fact is that I don't know what I should do. Should one not have an aim in life?'

'An aim in life,' I replied, 'is always better than a so-called ideal.'

'Always better,' said Tunda, 'if it is really an aim.'

We discovered that Irene had stayed at the Bellevue Hotel for three weeks and had then left for Paris.

'I shall go there,' said Tunda.

XXIII

The idea occurred to him to have his Siberian stories published. The book was unfinished. I wrote an epilogue in which I stated that the author had disappeared in

Siberia, and that the manuscript had come into my possession in some miraculous fashion. It appeared under the name of Baranowicz, in Tunda's translated version. It was brought out by a large Berlin publishing house.

I still recall how amazed Tunda was by the streets, the houses, how he noted improbable incidents and activities because to him even the ordinary appeared remarkable. He sat on the tops of buses. He stood before each of the hundred ghastly wooden posts which indicate direction or bar entry in Berlin. He possessed the uncanny capacity of seizing the uncannily sensible frenzy of this city. He had almost forgotten Irene.

'This city,' he said, 'exists outside Germany, outside Europe. It is its own capital. It does not draw its supplies from the land. It obtains nothing from the earth on which it is built. It converts this earth into asphalt, bricks and walls. It shades the plain with its houses, it supplies the plain with bread from its factories, it determines the plain's dialect, its national mores, its national costume. It is the very embodiment of a city. The country owes its existence to it, and expresses its gratitude by becoming absorbed by it. It has its own animal kingdom in the Zoological Gardens and the Aquarium, the Aviary and the Monkey House, its own vegetation in the Botanic Garden, its own stretches of sand on which foundations are laid and factories erected, it even has its own harbour, its river is a sea, it is a continent. Of all the cities I have seen, this one alone has humanity – for lack of time and other practical reasons. Many more people would perish here if it were not for a thousand cautious, circumspect measures to defend life and health, created not because of any dictates of the heart but because an accident interferes with the traffic, costs money, and offends against order. This city had the courage to be built in an ugly style, and this inclines it to further ugliness. It places signposts, boards, hoardings, loathsome, glassy, internally illuminated toads on the roadsides, at the intersections, on the squares. Its traffic police stand there with metal signals which look as if they were on temporary loan from the railway administration, and use them wearing spectral white gloves.

'What is more, it still tolerates the German provinces as part of itself, if only in order to devour them one day. It nourishes the natives of Düsseldorf, of Cologne, of Breslau, and draws nourishment from them. It has no culture of its own as have Breslau, Cologne, Frankfurt, Königsberg. It has no religion. It has the most hideous churches in the world. It has no society. But it has everything that society alone provides in every other city: theatres, art, a stock-exchange, trade, cinema, subways.'

In the course of a few days we saw: a man running amok and a procession; a film premiere, filming on location, the death leap of an artist in the Unter den Linden, the victim of an assault, the centre for the homeless, a love-scene in the Tiergarten in broad daylight, revolving advertising pillars turned by donkeys, thirteen clubs for homosexual and lesbian couples, a shy normal couple of between fourteen and sixteen who had carved their names on the trees and had their names taken by a park attendant because they had damaged public property, a man who had to pay a fine because he had walked diagonally across a square instead of at right angles, a meeting of the onion-eating sect and of the Salvation Army.

I also conducted my friend Tunda to the café where the artists met.

This was the time when literary men, actors, film-producers and painters were once more making money. It was the time following the stabilization of the German currency, when new bank-accounts were being opened, when even the most radical journals carried well-paid advertisements, and when radical writers earned honoraria in the literary supplements of the bourgeois papers. The world was so firmly back on its feet that even the *feuilletons* dared to be revolutionary; civil war was now so remote that revolutionary writers contemplated lawsuits and public prosecutors with a certain gratification and took their threats as friendly compliments.

I pointed out all the famous personalities to Tunda: the writer who sat there with beautiful prematurely bleached hair, his head silvered as if by a jeweller, the originator of gentle spitefulnesses in a style compounded in equal measure of good taste and the avoidance of sentimentality; the publisher of a journal who tendered his kindness of heart to all and sundry – even those who were not particularly interested – exhibited a commonplace masculine conceit instead of literary ambition, and was endowed with a great aptitude for stock-exchange transactions, making money and campaigning against big business. The famous artist of mediocre talent, who went on drawing the various celebrities until they had no option but to reflect their own lustre onto him. The revolutionary author of revolutionary tales who, a victim of the law, had spent three months in jail for freedom, for justice, for a new world, without securing anything but his own, not unwelcome, notoriety.

I showed Tunda the young people, a self-perpetuating throng greeting those already present with the arrogance of late arrivals, discussing foreign successes in order to promote their own, wearing monocles and coloured cravats, calling to mind the progeny of rich bankers, and oscillating indecisively between being the grandsons of Jewish grandmothers or the illegitimate sons of Hohenzollern princes.

I showed Tunda all those who look down on me, and whom I have to acknowledge because I make my living as a writer.

The following day Tunda sent money to his wife in Baku and to Baranowicz at Irkutsk. He wrote Baranowicz a detailed letter.

I was not to meet him again until the 27th of August, in Paris.

XXIV

He arrived in Paris on the 16th of May, at seven in the morning.

He had seen the sunrise. Over a landscape of dark green, in which the familiar deciduous forests showed up like cypress groves, a glowing sphere rolled aloft as if taken with a slow-motion camera and faded visibly.

Tunda felt as if he had seen the sun rise for the first time. Always before it had climbed out of those mists which obscure the transition from night to day and make a mystery of the dawn. But this time night and day seemed to him sharply demarcated from each other by a few neat bands of cloud on which the dawn mounted as if up a staircase.

He had expected a clear blue morning sky in Paris. But the morning in Paris is drawn with a soft pencil. The dispersed smoke of factories blends with the invisible residues of silvery gas lamps and hangs above the façades of the houses.

In every city of the world, at seven in the morning, it is the women who are the first to emerge: servant-girls and typists. In every city Tunda had so far seen, it was the women who carried with them out into the streets an aura of love, of night, of beds and of dreams. But the Parisian women who set foot in the morning streets seemed to have forgotten the night. On their lips and faces they wore fresh new make-up which miraculously resembled a sort of morning dew. These women were as perfectly dressed as if they were going to the theatre. Instead, they walked with calm bright eyes into a calm bright day. They walked fast, on sturdy legs and sound feet which seemed to know how to deal with paving-stones. As Tunda watched them walk he had the impression that they never used either their soles or their heels.

He passed through ugly old alleys with torn-up paving and cheap shops. But when he lifted his gaze above the shop-signs, they were palaces which suffered tradesmen at their feet with unconcerned indifference. There were always the same old window-panes, divided into eight parallelograms, the same grey, thin-grooved, half-lowered blinds. Only rarely was a window open, and rarely did an unclothed person stand at an open window.

In front of the shops sat cats; they waved their tails like flags. Like watchdogs, they sat with carefully obser-vant eyes over the crates of green lettuces and yellow turnips, lustrous bluish cabbages and rose-pink radishes. The shops looked like vegetable gardens and, despite the soft, lead-coloured atmosphere which veiled the sun, despite the smoke and heat suddenly rising from the asphalt, Tunda felt as if he were wandering in open country and smelled the odours rising from the ground.

He came to a small, circular, open place with a ridiculous monument in the middle. In fact, when he saw this monument he laughed out so loudly that he thought people would emerge from their houses. But not even those who were already there took any notice of him. They were a stout dark woman, who was standing before a milliner's, and a tall man with a glossy black moustache who was just opening up his small chocolate shop. They conversed, appeared to see Tunda but deliberately ignored him. They cracked jokes in the early morning. Tunda laughed in front of the monument.

It portrayed a smooth-shaven man in a flowing overcoat, life-size, on a pedestal. That death had not interrupted his everyday life seemed self-evident. A minor disturbance, nothing more. Comfortably settled in the centre of the circus instead of embarking on the long road to the next world, a small theatre with classical columns in the background, he continued to pursue his vocation, namely poetry.

The open space, except for its two shops, was still asleep. The houses gently encircled it as a ring does a finger. From various openings alleys radiated outwards in all directions, and one of these intimated the gleaming dark green proximity of a park, resonant with birdsong.

At the corner was an hotel, an hotel like a shop.

Tunda went inside, it was dark, a bell whimpered, and a made-up young woman emerged from behind a cheap flowered curtain. She appeared bold, worthy of respect, because she had the courage to live in darkness behind this curtain, because she asked Tunda what he wanted in a tone that was unfeeling, almost aggressive and yet kind. She seemed to him bold indeed, she seemed to have the splendid gift of passing through dreams as a creature of flesh and blood, and to be herself a miracle in the midst of miracles.

In this hotel, and because of this woman, Tunda rented a room on the sixth floor. From the window he could see the stone poet's soft hat, the sparrows dancing on his head, the theatre roof with its three-cornered jutting gable, all the radiating streets, the dark green of the garden on the right, and chimneys springing up far and wide like children in a blue haze.

In the afternoon he walked through streets large and small, broad and narrow, in which the terraces of cafés blossomed with small round tables on slender legs, and waiters moved about like gardeners; when they poured coffee and milk into the cups, it was as if they were watering white flower beds. Trees and kiosks stood on the kerbs, almost as if the trees were selling newspapers. In the shop-windows – he thought of the foolish shop-windows of the Rue de la Paix – the wares danced in what looked like apparent confusion, but was in fact a defined and regular pattern. The policemen strolled in the streets, yes, they strolled, a small cape over their right or left shoulder – it was remarkable that this article of clothing could protect against hail and cloudburst. Yet they wore it with an imperturbable confidence in the quality of the material or in the benevolence of the heavens – who can tell? They strolled, not like policemen, but like idlers with all the time in the world.

Tunda had the impression that, if he asked one of them where Irene might be, he would get an answer or, at least, some good advice. Irene lived in this city. Madame G. lived in this city. From the moment he had set foot in Paris he could no longer distinguish clearly between the two women. They were *one* woman and he loved her. He decided to write to Madame G.

He knew her address. He had copied it a dozen times; and, moreover, there lay in a compartment of his wallet the fatal scrap of paper with which she had betrayed herself.

He had bought new, soft, smooth writing-paper; he felt that with this paper he entered on a new period in his life. Much depends on these things; momentous letters, fateful letters, must be written on a pleasing attractive, animating, cheerful, festive kind of paper. He wrote this letter in violet ink in order to distinguish it from all other, ordinary letters. Above all, he had a confession to make to Madame G., one which might possibly disillusion her.

When he began to write, he had the feeling that the French language, especially, was made for confessions. Nothing easier than to be sincere in French. The naked truth, which always has a brutal ring, nestles softly yet clearly defined in its phraseology; it is visible rather than audible, as is fitting for the truth. The letter certainly had its faults; but no language lends itself to such noble, such ready-to-be-forgiven mistakes as does French. By the time he had sealed the letter and carefully inscribed the address, he was almost as audacious as his painted young *hotelière*.

Several days passed. No answer came. He waited. But this period of waiting was not accompanied by anxiety or apprehension, it was more like waiting in front of the lowered curtain at a theatre.

He stayed indoors most of the day. In the late mornings he was woken by a noise from the street which recurred regularly every day and whose origin he could not bring himself to determine. He was curious. He wanted to see what it was that he heard every morning. But he put it off from one day to the next; it was pleasant that he could voluntarily postpone it, and the ability to master his curiosity released a real and unsuspected feeling of power.

A servant came to clean his room even though Tunda was still in bed. This servant seemed to have been employed in the hotel for decades, and yet he performed his duties with considerable and startling zeal; he considered each speck of dust with curious satisfaction, he investigated the underside of the wash-basin as if he hoped to discover something unexpected there. Every morning he said: 'It's fine today, you should take a walk in the park!' And every morning Tunda replied: 'I'm expecting an important letter.' He spoke to Tunda like a kind uncle to an obstinate nephew, or like a gentle asylum attendant to a well-behaved patient. This servant was both ironic and courteous, although he liked to act the innocent and always bluntly told the truth. 'How you do enjoy your sleep!' he once said. And the longer Tunda slept, the oftener he excused himself: 'Forgive me, I've woken you up!'

One day he arrived earlier than usual, brandished a blue envelope, and exclaimed: 'Here's the letter you've been waiting for!' He laid it on the counterpane and withdrew his hand rapidly as if the paper was burning him, as if it might explode at any moment. It was a cheap, transparent, ordinary envelope, it felt like blotting-paper, and it contained the bill.

On that day Tunda went out for the second time; he sat down in the nearby park opposite a pond on which boys were sailing small boats. He wanted to induce a letter to arrive. The letter must be outwitted. If it was not allowed to know how impatiently it was awaited, then it would certainly arrive.

But no letter arrived.

Once more Tunda asked the young woman if anyone had been asking for him. And just like the first time she said with a consolatory toss of the head – it was like the cold professional sympathy of an undertaker – 'The last post hasn't been yet; the postman comes around seven o'clock.'

But nothing came with the last post either.

It was morning again, the familiar unknown noise woke Tunda, the servant entered, he was still chewing his breakfast. Suddenly, as he began lovingly to polish the water-tap, he said:

'Someone was asking after you yesterday.'

'Who? When? What time? A lady?'

'It was around five in the afternoon . . .'

And he pulled out a thick silver watch on a thick silver chain, studied it for a few seconds as if he had remarked something on the dial, and repeated:

'Yes, at five in the afternoon.'

'And who was it?'

'A lady.'

'Didn't she leave anything?'

'No.'

'A young lady?'

'Yes, it was a young lady actually.'

'And didn't she say whether she'd come back?'

'Not to me.'

'To whom then?'

'To no one.'

Then he burnished the tap even more thoroughly, threw the soap in the air like a ball and caught it again, laughed and said:

'A pretty little young lady.'

'And did she speak only to you?'

'Yes, only to me.'

'And why didn't you say so yesterday?'

'It was my evening off yesterday. I went for a stroll.'

'Here's a tip. And if she comes again, tell me before you go for your stroll.'

The man tossed the gold piece in the air as he had done the soap and said: 'Forgive me if I've inconvenienced you,' and departed.

Then came a long Saturday, the servant brought new bed-linen and towels, he stroked them before hanging them over the arm of one of the chairs, and turned to go. He held the door-handle for a moment, hesitated as if he had something important yet embarrassing to say.

Suddenly, already halfway through the door, he spoke:

'No one has been.'

Tunda awoke in broad daylight on Sunday morning.

The sky was just above the window, small white clouds drifted by, it was indisputably May in the world.

There was a knock on the door and the servant said:

'There's someone to speak to you . . .'

Madame G. entered.

She slowly stripped off a glove, it fell on the counterpane, lightly, deposited by a soft breeze. It lay there, empty, flaccid, but like a tender, living, curious animal.

'Well, my friend,' she said, 'have you come here to see me or to prepare for the Revolution?'

'To see you! Do you still not believe me? Everything I wrote to you is true. I swear it!'

Tunda held out his papers, as if she were from the police, as if he had to defend his freedom.

She sat down on the bed – and it was like a miracle. She scratched at the papers with three fingers, regarded them disdainfully, and immediately extracted Irene's photograph.

'Who's this beautiful woman?'

'She was my fiancée.'

'And she is dead?' she asked in a tranquil voice. Nothing was simpler in the world than Irene's death. Not just Irene, all women were dead, buried.

'I think she's still alive,' said Tunda timidly, as if begging her pardon.

He kissed her hand, she put a cigarette in her mouth with her left hand, and he jumped up to fetch some matches.

Suddenly it seemed that nothing in the entire world was as important as these matches. The match burned, a small, blue, festal fire.

'Goodbye!' she said, but did not look at him, only at Irene's photograph which still lay on the bed.

The sky was still blue.

XXV

Tunda had a few letters of introduction from his brother and from acquaintances. He paid calls.

They were calls of the most tedious nature. There were learned and semi-learned men, worthy, but with a worth adulterated by wit. There were men with smooth, old, well-preserved faces and carefully brushed grey beards which still showed the marks of the comb. These men, holders of public offices, were professors or authors or presidents of humanitarian or so-called cultural associations. For thirty years they had had little else to do than to keep up appearances. They were distinguished from their German colleagues by their precise, rounded, polished gestures and their polite manner of speech.

Tunda got to know the President Marcel de K. He lived in a Parisian suburb, in a villa which he left only two or three times a year to attend special ceremonial sessions of the Academy.

He assured Tunda of his love for Germany.

'Mr President,' said Tunda, 'you do me great honour in assuring me, a private person, of your esteemed love for Germany. But I am hardly in a position to accept your cordial assurances. I am not a public servant, not even a private one. I would find it embarrassing if I were asked to tell you what my occupation was. I returned from Russia not long ago, and have barely had time to look around in Germany. I spent two weeks in Berlin and stayed only a little longer with my brother in the town of X. on the Rhine. I did not even have time to find my bearings in Austria, my home country.'

He had caused the venerable old gentleman a certain embarrassment. So he added: 'However, I could tell you about Siberia, if that interests you.'

They spoke of Russia. The President had the impression that the shooting was still going on in St Petersburg.

Tunda came to realize that the President's refined tastes permitted him every kind of ignorance. He had the right to know absolutely nothing. France gave him everything he needed: mountains, sea, mystery, clarity, nature, art, science, revolution, religion, history, pleasure, grace and tragedy, beauty, wit, satire, enlightenment and reaction.

Tunda regarded the old gentleman with the pure delight experienced by some people when they stroll in a well-kept garden. He contemplated his elderly regular features, on which sorrow had acted with discretion; disappointments lay in predetermined furrows; the minor pleasures of life had left a fine, clear brightness in the eyes; round the thin, sharp lips and wide mouth the beard was spread in its silver repose; the head had lost only so much hair as was necessary to display a fine, intelligent, distinguished forehead. What an elder! No one could be more entitled to the name of President than he.

Tunda had adopted the habit of mistrusting beauty. Thus, initially, he did not believe a single word the President said, not even the most insignificant. When, for instance, he related how, twenty years before, he had taken some Minister or other aside in the Chamber of Deputies, in order to tell him the truth in private, Tunda took this for an exaggeration, an indulgence of his old age. For the truths M. de K. had to tell could have been uttered in public without fear of possible consequences.

But after he had conversed with this friendly gentleman three or four times, he began to suspect that the old man in no wise exaggerated. He did not overstate the facts, merely the degree and dangers of his truthfulness. That which, with a certain *frisson*, he called the truth, was an equivocal, almost a ridiculous, aspect of the truth. He certainly did not consciously exaggerate. If he expressed some commonplace, oft-repeated remark of abysmal banality about Germany, it was no thoughtless repetition in his mouth, but something like a polite discovery. Time and time again he relived the experiences of the past. When he said paternally: 'I value your society, my dear young man,' Tunda was compelled to feel himself really singled out. In this circumspect mouth, because of the slow movements of the tongue, every phrase acquired its old and original meaning. And it was plain that the old gentleman had to see a Minister n private in order to be able to tell him : 'I have clearly noted the double meaning of your speech.'

Tunda learned from this man's example that an important aspect of a distinguished bearing is fear of exaggeration (even the unadorned truth is an exaggeration) and a faith in the aptness and the appropriateness of tried and tested phrases. For him any new turn of phrase overstepped the mark.

At the worthy President's he made the acquaintance of a number of persons : the editor of an 'important' newspaper; his colleagues; a woman to whose relations with a Minister allusions were made; a nobleman who hailed from the Rhine and had relatives in ruined castles in France, Italy and Austria. He was one of those aristocrats who publish magazines in order to prove themselves worthy of their illustrious names by means of a species of creative activity. They have not yet come to terms with the accepted impotence of the aristocracy, and while they allay their appetites at the tables of their successors, the industrialists, they never for a moment forget that they adorn these tables at the same time. Because, unlike many of their fellows, they do not even possess the ability to distinguish themselves as factory directors or personnel managers in coal-mining areas, they busy themselves with politics. And because they can no longer hope to increase their possessions through war, they indulge in the politics of peace. Moreover, the particular charm of the man under discussion lay in the fact that he was in favour of a dictatorship, of the iron hand. He looked forward to a united Europe under the dominion of a Pope with the temporal power of a dictator, or something of the kind. When he spoke, he placed his hands together so that the fingertips touched; he must at some time have learnt this habit of making steeples out of hands from a priest. He spoke with the persuasive, soft and sonorous voice of a professional hypnotist and clothed sober statements with a mystic radiance. Beyond that, he readily made himself out to be a poor devil – even this can be an attraction in good society.

The wives of rich manufacturers, who always think themselves misunderstood, but have little opportunity to acquire close contact with literature – because literary men can on occasion be quite dangerous – surrender willingly to aristocrats with literary leanings, where the female soul finds everything it needs : understanding, tenderness, nobility, a dash of bohemianism. This man not only ate at the tables of the industrialists, he slept in their beds. In the irregular intervals between, he published his magazine. He had collaborators in every camp, for even honourable men exist who take an interest in the peace of Europe.

As, for example, the diplomat who was employed at the French Embassy in Berlin, and had staked his career on a Franco-German entente. He had lived in Germany for years and cordially hated it. But what could this hate avail against self-love? Every step towards the so-called *rapprochement* was counted in his favour, he achieved results against his will, he was a specialist in Germanophilia.

More honest, but more ignorant, too, was the lady with the connections. Apart from a friendly face and a statuesque figure, she possessed only as much intellect as was required for a newspaper article or a discussion with a German Minister.

At solemn moments they all spoke of a community of European culture. Once Tunda asked :

'Do you think you could manage to tell me precisely

what constitutes this culture which you claim to defend, even though it is in no way threatened from outside?'

'Religion!' said the President, who never went to church.

'Morality,' said the lady, whose irregular associations were common knowledge.

'Art,' said the diplomat, who had never looked at a picture since his schooldays.

'The European idea,' said someone by the name of Rappaport – diplomatically, because he was in every way a gentleman.

The aristocrat, however, contented himself with the remark: 'Just read my magazine!'

'You want,' said Tunda, 'to uphold a European community, but you must first establish it. For this community does not exist, otherwise it would already know how to maintain itself. All in all, it seems to me very doubtful whether anyone can establish anything at all. And who would attack this culture anyway, even if it did exist? Official Bolshevism, perhaps? Even though Russia wants it, too?'

'But may want to destroy it here – especially here – in order to be the sole possessor,' exclaimed M. Rappaport.

'Before that happens, it will probably have succumbed to another war.'

'That is exactly what we are seeking to prevent,' several persons said simultaneously.

'And wasn't that what you wanted in 1914, too? But when war broke out, you went to Switzerland and published journals, while here they were shooting conscientious objectors. You certainly have the means to buy a ticket to Zürich at the right moment, and the right contacts to obtain a valid passport. But do the people? A workman, even in peacetime, must wait three days for a visa. It's only the call-up papers that arrive on time.'

'You are a pessimist,' said the benevolent President.

At that moment a gentleman, already known to Tunda, entered the room. It was M. de V., who had just returned from an American tour. He was still a secretary, though no longer with the lawyer but with an eminent politician.

He had never expected, he said, that Tunda would really ever come to Paris. And what a happy chance that brought them together at his old and dear friend's — as he felt he could well call the President!

Then the secretary began to talk about America.

He was a 'born raconteur'. He took as his starting point some vivid and exaggerated situation, and proceeded from personal experiences to conditions in general. He raised and lowered his voice, he related the essential very softly so that he might drown non-essentials with a loud voice. He gave detailed descriptions of the traffic in the streets and the efficient hotels. He ridiculed the Americans. He described stage productions with malice. He made intimate innuendoes about the women. Each time he tugged at the trouser creases at his knees; from a distance it looked like a young girl shyly pulling at her apron. The secretary was unquestionably a sympathetic person. But the effect of his sudden return from America was that the benevolent old President no longer invited Tunda so frequently, and no longer addressed him as 'Dear Sir' but as 'Sir'.

XXVI

At Madame G.'s Tunda was able to meet the intimate friend of a great poet, together with other individuals.

The ladies sat with their hats on; an older lady did not remove her gloves. She accepted a small pastry with her leather fingers, inserted it between carmined lips, chewed it with porcelain teeth; whether her palate was real remained dubious. But it was not she, but the friend of the great poet, who attracted attention.

The poet's friend, a Hungarian, had acclimatized himself in Paris as he once had in Budapest. The Hungarian accent with which he sang in French would have offended the sensitive ears of the French, had he not portrayed in these melodies episodes from the life of his great literary friend. Also, the Hungarian was a cultural peddler and polyglot from birth. He could even make his living at it; for he translated Molnar, Anatole France, Proust and Wells – each into the language required for the occasion, and fashionable comedies into all languages alike. He was known in the press gallery of the League of Nations at Geneva, as well as in the offices of the Berlin *Revuetheater*, theatrical agents and the editorial staffs of all the literary supplements of the great continental newspapers.

He spoke like a flute. It was wonderful how his delicate throat was able to further the interests of his Hungarian friends at the League for Human Rights. He did, in fact, accomplish a lot of good, not from any innate helpfulness but because he was compelled by his connections to be obliging.

It happened that he and Tunda left Madame G.'s house at the same time. He was one of those Middle European men who take the person they are conversing with by the arm and stand still or stop talking at every street-corner. They fall silent if the other withdraws his arm, just as an electric light goes out if the plug is pulled out of the wall.

'Do you know M. de V.?' he asked.

'Not very well,' replied Tunda.

'What a capable man! Imagine, he has just got back from America. A trip round the world is nothing to him. He's seen half the world already anyway. And it doesn't cost him a penny. He's always employed by some rich or at least influential man. As a secretary or – '

He waited a long minute, then said : 'It's all over with Madame G.'

He released Tunda's arm and stood facing him as if expecting something extraordinary.

Instead Tunda said nothing.

'But I dare say you knew that?' he asked.

'No.'

'Then you're not interested in the gentleman?'

'Not especially.'

'Then let's go and have some coffee.'

And they went to have some coffee.

XXVII

About this time Tunda's money began to run out.

He wrote to his brother. George replied that unfortunately he was unable to help with ready cash. Of course, his house was always open.

The boldness of the beautiful *hotelière*, which had so impressed Tunda, turned into derision. For beautiful, young bold hotel manageresses do not spend their lives behind gloomy, cheap, floral curtains for nothing. They expect some payment in return.

They regard the poverty of a tenant as malicious cunning, aimed at them personally by the tenant.

The conception the lower middle class has of poverty is that the poor man diligently courts it in order to inflict injury on his neighbour.

But it is precisely the lower middle class on whom the man who has nothing depends. High up behind the clouds lives God, whose infinite bounty has become proverbial. A little lower live those pampered individuals who are comfortably off, and who are so immune to any contagion from poverty that they develop those powerful virtues : sympathy for the needy, compassion, benevolence, and even freedom from prejudice. But squeezed between these noble folk and the others who need generosity most urgently, acting as insulators as it were, are the middle classes who trade in bread and provide food and lodging. The entire 'social problem' would be solved if only the rich, who are in a position to give away a loaf, were also the world's bakers. There would be far less injustice if the jurists of the highest tribunals were to sit in the small criminal courts, and if police commissioners had personally to arrest petty thieves.

But life is not like that.

The hotel servant was the first to sense that Tunda's money had run out. In the course of a long life he had developed his natural instinct for the fortunes of a fluctuating clientele to prophetic dimensions. He had seen millions of razor-blades grow blunt, millions of cakes of soap grow smaller, millions of toothpaste tubes go flat. He had seen a thousand suits make their exodus from the wardrobes. He had learned to recognize whether a man was returning hungry from the park or satisfied from a restaurant.

XXVIII

Tunda still did not know Europe. He had fought for a year and a half for a great Revolution. But only now did it become clear to him that revolutions were not waged against the 'bourgeoisie' but against bakers, against waiters, against small greengrocers, insignificant butchers and defenceless hotel servants.

He had never feared poverty, barely experienced it. But in the capital of the European world, the source of all the ideas and songs about freedom, he saw that even a dry crust is not to be had for nothing. There are specific sources of charity for beggars; every compassionate individual who is appealed to will put up the engaged sign!

He went once to see Madame G.

For the first time it occurred to him that there was nothing whatever between her and himself, that that afternoon, that evening in Baku, meant no more than the encounter of two persons at a railway station before they board different trains. He realized that her capacity to experience, to feel sorrow, joy, anguish, grief, ecstasy or anything that goes to make up life, had become extinct. He could not decide whether it was her possessions, the material security in which she lived, that had made her apathetic. She had the admirable and mysterious gift of touching objects and people with slender fingers and the ground with beautiful narrow feet and toes. So her every movement had its meaning, a remote, a poetic meaning, which remained outside and yet transcended any immediate purpose. She contained within herself that domain of European culture discussed by those averters of calamity, the Europeans. There was no need for any other, any more convincing evidence for the existence of a European culture than this Madame G. But to guarantee her existence, people were heartless, bakers obdurate, and the poor without bread. And she, the product of these misfortunes, did not know, was not allowed to know, was not even allowed to experience a great passion because passion is noxious to beauty. Nevertheless, the world was not as simple as Natasha had once declared. There are other antitheses than between rich and poor. But there is a kind of poverty to which one owes a multitude of experiences, even life itself, and a kind of abundance which renders everything lifeless – lifeless and beautiful, lifeless and enchanting, lifeless, happy and finite.

As though by some obligatory decree, Tunda said: 'I love you!', perhaps merely to announce his presence.

For what else was there for him to seek here? Like a man who loses someone, he was driven to seek – by that instinct which is sometimes stronger than the instinct of self-preservation – some last means of keeping her.

All the time he wondered what she would say if he took the liberty of asking her for money. How repulsive it would be to her, first, that he had no money, second, that he mentioned it in her presence, third, that his most immediate worry was what he was going to eat the next day! How she would despise him! How loathsome is the money we do not have! And how much more loathsome when we need it from a beautiful woman in the heart of the most beautiful city in the world. In her eyes, poverty was the epitome of unmanliness – and not in her eyes alone. This was the world where poverty meant lack of masculinity, weakness, folly, cowardice and depravity.

He left her with that forced and hopeless gaiety which resembles the smile of a tired vaudeville artist, with the gaiety we assume a hundred times a day, as if we were taking our bows before an audience. He departed from her quietly, like one bent on suicide from a loved and despised existence.

He walked the length of the Rue de Berri, in which she lived, reached the Champs Elysées, and found himself brushing against people yet feeling quite detached from them. It was as if he was standing outside the world like a beggar, looking at it only through a hard, impenetrable pane of glass, menacing despite its friendliness.

It was a bright afternoon; the little motorcars careered along the broad streets like straying children, playful, cheerful and noisy. Handsome old gentlemen strolled about, light gloves on their hands, light spats on their feet, but the rest of their clothing was dark – they looked both solemn and cheerful. They were going to the Bois de Boulogne to spend the evening of their lives there – a merry evening, like a second dawn. Little girls walked along, well-bred, mature, sagacious metropolitan children who lead their mothers by the hand and wander over the pavement with the graceful assurance of grown ladies – fabulous creatures, half-animal, half-princess. On the terraces sat the real grown-up ladies, yellow stalks like slender flutes between their red lips. The world lay behind glass, as old and precious tapestries lie in a museum, hovering on the point of disintegration.

Tunda encountered the friend of the great poet, for it was the hour in Paris when those who belong to a certain social stratum throng the Champs Elysées – that is, if one is permitted to apply the word 'throng' to the strolling of these ladies and gentlemen.

It was as if they were being led by someone, as animals in a zoo or in a menagerie can be led around at certain times of the day; it was like opening a section of a museum for a few hours in the week to afford a special view of some rare and ancient precious objects.

Who directed these people? Who displayed them in this museum called the Champs Elysées, who bade them walk and turn around like mannequins? Who brought them together in the salons of the Presidents and at the tea-parties of the beautiful women? How did the great poets come to their friends and the friends to the great poets? How did M. de V. come to the President?

Not by accident but by decree.

Ah, the things they did! At times they seemed to Tunda like grave-worms, the world was their coffin, but there was no one in the coffin. The coffin lay in the ground and the worms bored tunnels through the wood, bored holes, came together, bored further until the coffin became one great hole and worms and coffin were no more, while the earth was astonished that no corpse had been laid therein.

XXIX

One day Tunda made up his mind to ask the worthy President for help. He had hesitated for some weeks. For he did not know whether it would be better to write a frank, albeit brief and polite, letter to the old gentleman – who probably weighed his own actions very carefully and had never allowed himself to step even slightly out of line – or to pay him a visit.

Tunda discovered that all his experience did not suffice to give him assurance in a world where he was not at home. All at once he understood the timidity of invalids, those invalids who lose their eyes, ears, noses and legs in the purgatory of war and, back home again, obey the order of a servant-girl who turns them away from the front-door. His heart was beating. Whatever courage and vigour he had once been able to summon up had been only in response to some particular situation; cowardice was the condition of domesticated men.

He wrote several letters and tore them up again. He made an effort to recall the red nights, the flaming crimson of those vanished days, the immense, limitless, absolute whiteness of the Siberian ice, the tremendous silence of the forests through which he had wandered and in which nothing was audible but the breath of death, the choking hunger which had gnawed at his vitals, his perilous flight, and the day when he was slung over the back of a galloping horse, the moment when he lost consciousness – like a sudden and yet gradual descent into a dark-red gulf of softness, terror and death. But his recollections were of no avail. For the present is a thousand times more compelling than the most compelling past – and he could understand the suffering of persons who heroically endured a dangerous operation ten years ago and are overwhelmed by a present toothache.

He decided to call on the President. He had not given notice of his arrival and as he stood at the door he found some consolation in thinking that he could occupy the first two minutes with excuses for his sudden visit. To which the President would certainly reply, with his accustomed and beautifully convincing cordiality, that he was especially delighted that Tunda should visit him. Then Tunda would summon up the courage to dis-illusion him.

M. le President was at home, and he was alone. Once again Tunda admired the precise, unsuspecting and inexorable protocol, the formality which was never for a moment interrupted, which was unconcerned with the purpose of his visit, according him the same respect that was due to an independent, proud and free individual. The servant still treated him politely today; tomorrow, when he had finally and visibly sunk into the wretched category of rejected supplicant, he would refuse him admission just as imperturbably. There are no excep-tions. Tunda thought of the decree of which the tipsy manufacturer had once spoken. One may have long since accomplished one's escape from class, position, social category, but the protocol is still unaware of this, and before it has registered either an ascent or descent, this and that detail may no longer be true. Tunda was like a man who comes from an earthquake stricken city and is received by those who know nothing about it as if he had just descended from a train arriving on schedule.

But if ante-room and servant still seemed to him as in former times – how suddenly the few weeks had lengthened into decades! – he perceived in the President's gaze the whole alteration in his own position. For the owners of property, the serene, the untroubled, yes, even those only modestly provided for, develop a defensive instinct against any invasion of their protected territory, they shun even the slightest contact with one from whom they may expect a request and scent the proximity of helplessness with the certainty of prairie animals detecting a forest fire. The President would have divined the change in Tunda's condition; and even if he had been known to him up till then as a millionaire and fellow clubman of the Citroëns, he would have divined it at the very moment when Tunda approached him to avow his poverty – the President would have divined it, thanks to the prophetic gift that goes with property, security, the bourgeois condition, as the sheepdog accompanies the blind brushmaker.

The President's nobility was transformed into fear, his reserve into severity, his prudence into peevishness. Yes, even his handsomeness was now revealed as cheap, superficial, easily explicable vanity. His beautiful silver beard was the product of a brush and comb, his smooth brow an index of thoughtless and complacent egoism, his well-tended fingernails the counterpart of sophisticated claws, his gaze the expression of a glassily smooth eye that received images of the world as indifferently as a mirror.

'I'm in a bad way, M. le President!' said Tunda.

The President's expression became even graver and

he indicated a comfortable leather armchair, like a doctor prepared to listen and to take in the details with the cheerful interest medical men show in a case-history which might further their studies. He sat there like God the Father, shaded as in a cloud, while a broad beam of sunlight fell through the window onto Tunda so that his knees were illuminated and the light stood before him like a golden transparent wall behind which the President sat and listened, or did not listen. But then a remarkable thing came to pass; the President arose, the wall of crystalline gold advanced towards him, he broke through it, it turned into a golden veil which conformed to the shape of his body, lay on his shoulders and showed up a little white scurf on his blue suit. The President stood there, human now, extended a hand to Tunda, and said: 'Perhaps I can do something for you.'

XXX

Tunda walked through the bright streets with a great void in his heart, feeling like a released convict on his first emergence to freedom. He knew that the President could not help him, even if he made it possible for him to eat and to buy a suit. As little as one makes a convict free by releasing him from prison. As little as one renders a parentless child happy by finding him a place in an orphanage. He was not at home in this world. Where then? In the mass graves.

The blue light shone on the grave of the Unknown Soldier. The wreaths withered. Young Englishmen stood there, soft grey hats in their hands, their hands behind their backs. They had left the Café de la Paix to visit the memorial. An old father thought of his son. Between him and the young Englishmen lay the tomb. Deep under both lay the remains of the Unknown Soldier. The old man and the young ones exchanged glances over the tomb. There was a tacit understanding between them. It was as if they sealed a pact, not to join in mourning for the dead soldier, but to join in forgetting.

Tunda had already passed by this memorial a number of times. There were always tourists standing around, hat in hand, and nothing upset him more than their marks of respect. It was like globe-trotters, who happened also to be devout, visiting a famous church during a service and kneeling, guidebook in hand, before the altar, out of habit and in order not to incur self-reproach. Their devotion is a blasphemy and a ransom for their conscience. The blue flame burned under the Arc de Triomphe, not to honour the dead soldier but to reassure those who survived him. Nothing was more gruesome than the unsuspecting devotion of a surviving father at the tomb of his son, whom he had sacrificed without knowing it. Tunda sometimes felt as if he himself lay there in the ground, as if we all lay there, all those of us who set out from home and were killed and buried, or who came back but never again came home – for it is a matter of indifference whether we are buried or alive and well. We are strangers in this world, we come from the realm of the dead.

A few days later the President asked him to call.

Between the two there now existed that distance which exists between the man who gives help and the one who accepts it, a distance different from that between an older and a younger man, a native and a foreigner, someone powerful and someone who, though weak, is still independent. Although there was no contempt in the President's gaze, it no longer showed that quiet preparedness for respect, the open-minded hospitality, which distinguished people reserve for foreigners. It may be that Tunda had touched his heart. But they were no longer as free with each other as they had been. Perhaps, after this, the old man would have trusted Tunda with one of his secrets, but he would no longer trust him with one of his daughters.

'I have found something,' said the President. 'There is a M. Cardillac, whose daughter is taking a trip to Germany and needs a little conversational practice. The usual thing in such cases is to find some elderly lady from Alsace. But I am against that kind of teacher in principle because, though they certainly have a command of the language, it is quite another branch of the language – not at all what a young lady from a wealthy family requires. These teachers lack the necessary vocabulary. On the other hand I felt that a young man from a good background, a man of the world, knowledgeable and with much experience' – the list of Tunda's virtues grew noticeably – 'would be versed in exactly the right sort of parlance. It will also be a matter of explaining to the young lady the conditions in the areas she is about to visit, naturally quite objectively and without stirring up any preconceptions. Such prejudices would be all the worse since M. Cardillac – between ourselves, that is not his real name – has relations, distant relations naturally, in Germany – in Dresden and Leipzig if I am not mistaken.'

As if a President who supported peace in Europe and declared his esteem for Germany had to justify being acquainted with a M. Cardillac who owned German relations, the old man said:

'I don't know M. Cardillac very well. He was introduced to me some years ago. He comes from an old Milanese family which produces the world-famous tiled stoves, as well as common knick-knacks of all kinds. M. Cardillac is well-situated; he practises as an art-dealer, I believe, his contacts are more of a business than a social nature, but as you know, my dear sir,' he repeated, 'my dear sir' – 'since the war business and social life have become more or less identical . . .' And for a few moments the President lapsed into silence, into a restorative pause to allow himself time to recover from the self-administered shock of propounding the identity of commerce and society.

He certainly desired peace between nations, but what he understood by that was peace between certain social strata; he had no prejudices, he considered himself the most progressive member of the cultural world, but the categories he had created for himself were firmly based on the very prejudices he abjured. With those who are labelled 'reactionary', the President had a common foundation; his house was more airy, it had more windows, but it would collapse the moment its foundations were disturbed. He was certainly ashamed of his acquaintance with M. Cardillac. It was distasteful for him to have to speak of that gentleman. Perhaps he could just as easily have put Tunda in touch with some other, better-connected young lady. But then, Tunda no longer stood so high in his estimation since his appeal for help.

XXXI

Thus Tunda gained entrance to M. Cardillac's home.

He had never seen a larger house. It seemed to him even more spacious than it really was because he did not become fully acquainted with the whole of it, because – since he only managed to see parts or fragments of the house – he knew it as little as one knows a dictionary where one singles out a particular section from time to time in order to look up a particular word.

He was most interested in Mlle. Pauline, with whom he had to carry on conversation. Eighteen years old, with the familiar brown complexion of the Balkans – M. Cardillac originated from southern Rumania – a complexion reminiscent of the colour of meteorites and seeming to comprise iron, wind and sun, with sloping, meagre, pitiful shoulders, with soft, delicate hips threatened, in years to come, by a dangerously disfiguring breadth – Pauline seemed worthy of a better father than the one she had, and a wider, fuller life than the one she led. It was one of Tunda's fatal propensities to feel compassion for pretty women. To him their beauty seemed merely the proper index of their value, he could not get used to the idea that beauty is not some abundance of the female body, not grace or luxury, something akin to the genius of a masculine mind, but the self-evident tool of their existence, like their limbs, their head, their eyes. A woman's beauty is her single, yes her primary distinguishing feature, as the breast is the organ of her sexuality and her maternity. Most women are beautiful, just as most men are not cripples. But Tunda was disconcerted by this beauty to such an extent that he was inclined to seek an explanation for it in some inadequately appreciated virtue in its possessor. His love was always initiated by compassion, together with the compulsion to rid the world of an atrocious injustice.

At first, then, he overestimated Pauline. It gave him pleasure to see how she entered the room where he awaited her, how for a moment she left slightly ajar the door which led into her room, a room that seemed to be filled with indescribable, amorphous, purely ethereal extravagances. It delighted him to see how, with graceful helplessness, she placed her arm behind her back to shut the door, whose handle was level with her head. She did this as if she was trying to conceal something dangerous, known only to the two of them, so that every time it seemed for a moment as if they had a forbidden tryst. Her slender hands, scarcely trusting themselves to hold anything, were cool, a pale, fading red which lingered hesitantly on from Pauline's earlier adolescent years. She used these hands cautiously, as if they were precious limbs that she had been lent; Pauline was conscious of her hands only vaguely, as young birds are of their wings. She extended her arms too far, or she pressed her elbow too anxiously against her breast, she had not yet acquired experience in judging distances. Tunda appreciated the rounded quadrant of her recessed chin seen in profile, and the soft white down which entirely covered her russet face, a kind of silvery moss of youth and beauty.

Nevertheless, he remained aware that this girl, young and undeveloped as she was, came, like her adult counterparts from a world he despised and one which did not deserve its beauty. What kind of people had she been with; to what kind of people was she going? Her days and nights were filled with the ignominious and ridiculous ideas, conversation, experiences and emotions of these people. She went on outings with them, attended balls, visited mountains and spas, fell in love with them, played and danced with them, would marry one of them and bear children which looked as they all did. Reason enough to despise her! Reason enough to suppose that Nature, blind as she is, endows the women of this unnatural caste with beauty just as she makes its men grow straight and healthy. As a monk, exposed to the risk of being attracted by a woman, escapes this danger by means of the unnatural but infallible remedy of abstracting the woman from her charms, so Tunda began to relate Pauline to her world. Soon he found in the depths of her darting, flirtatious, yet always circumspect eyes, in those anatomically indeterminate, medically unfathomable depths, a blank screen against which the images of the world were sadly shattered.

He found in her smooth and well-ordered features the chill stupidity which so resembles charming good nature, unselfconscious grace and naïve joy in living. He found that same cheerless, enchanting, elegant stupidity that takes pity on pavement beggars yet tramples a thousand lives with each light step it takes.

It was a rich house. The young people who frequented it were as much at home in the Tattersalls and stadiums of the international sporting world as their fathers had been in the jewel markets from Bucharest to Amsterdam. But just as the slightly colour-blind are insensitive to part of the spectrum and cannot, or only with difficulty, tell violet from blue and blue from dark-green, so these young people lacked a feeling for the beauty, ugliness, naturalness, unnaturalness, charm and disgust of particular situations and particular circumstances. Yes, they lacked this totally. Most of all, Tunda was amazed that, although they were enthusiastic about nature and claimed – indeed believed themselves – to be at one with it, yet they were quite unaffected by nature's changing moods, exhibiting the same expression on dull, cold days as on warm and bright ones, always finding themselves in that specially animated, hectic and slightly perspiring condition common to participants and ballboys at tennis tournaments, whether in thundery oppression or after-rain freshness, at noon, at sunrise or at sunset. Whether in dinner-jackets or sports-shirts, they were the same. With strong, square, white teeth, like an advertisement for toothpaste, which they bared in place of a smile, with broadly-padded shoulders and narrow waists, with large muscular hands from which all tactile sense had been hygienically removed, with their coloured cravats round their necks, with tidily cut and well-tended hair which showed no hint of ever losing its colour, massaged, showered, always giving the impression of having just emerged from a sea-bathe, he encountered these young men as a species of urban domesticated beasts of prey, kept on the main boulevard, and cared for and supported by the municipality. They spoke with resounding voices, the echo already present within their oral cavities. With imperturbable seriousness they uttered the kind of polite phrases that are listed in the cheapest etiquette books. They were able to discuss every aspect of human life in the tone which the fashionable magazines employ when dutifully dealing with politics, literature and finance on their last pages, and in the smallest print, after a thorough discussion of the season's fashions. These young people discussed machines and motor-cars in the language of the classified advertisements. Indeed, they seemed to base their style on the advertisement sections of these magazines. They always knew exactly what to say about things and affairs, and what they said stood in roughly the same relation to these as a snapshot taken by an aerial photographer does to the facial expressions of a restive courting couple.

The female members of this society led a pleasure-orientated existence in thin, colourful, light expensive dresses. They walked the pavement on flawlessly shaped legs, in shoes of remarkable – often eccentric – cut, steered motorcars, galloped on horseback, drove light carriages, and called Claude Anet their favourite author. They never appeared singly or in pairs, but gathered in flocks like birds of passage and, like these birds, they were all equally beautiful. Among themselves they could probably be told apart by their particular clothes and bows, by the difference between certain hair-tints and lipstick colours; but to the observer they were children of the same mother, sisters of staggering similarity. The fact that they bore different names was an error of officialdom.

In addition, the majority had English first names. They had not – and this was perfectly reasonable – been called after saints or grandmothers, but after the heroines of American films or English drawing-room comedies. They had been perfectly equipped to take on their particular roles. When they entered a room, a cloud of fragrance and beauty drifting before them and spreading about them, they might be treading a stage or transforming themselves into moving shadows on a screen. It was self-evident that, though so vivacious, they had no life in them. Tunda perceived them not as realities, but as one perceives the girls of vaudeville shows – improbably alike, beautiful and numerous, a kind of daydream despite their sensual charm and physical liveliness – slotted in between the acts of comedians, the outcome of hypnotic suggestion. To Tunda all these girls seemed as unreal as the photographs in the illustrated magazines; when he encountered them, it was as if he had come upon them when turning over a page. And, in reality, they *were* the charming subjects of the illustrated magazines. They were, indeed, the greater half of the fashionable world, tobogganing in winter in the dazzling snows of St Moritz (gleaming white wool on their bodies), flower-wreathed in February in the carnival procession at Nice, naked on the seashore in summer, returning home in the autumn to inaugurate the winter season with their new hats.

They were all beautiful. They possessed the beauty of a species. It seemed as if their creator had distributed a great quantity of beauty among them all impartially; but it did not suffice to distinguish between them.

XXXII

Whenever Tunda thought of Irene, she seemed to him as far removed from this carefree and charming world as he was himself. One may call such an attitude 'romantic'. But it seems to me that this is the only attitude that has any validity today. It seems to me that there can no longer be any choice between enduring the torment of reality, of false categories, soulless concepts, amorphous schemata, and the pleasure of living in a fully accepted unreality. Given the choice between an Irene who played golf and danced the Charleston and one who was not even registered with the police, Tunda opted for the latter. But what gave him the right to expect a woman who was any different from all the others he saw? From Madame G., for instance, whom he had loved for an evening, the remote image of the remote Irene? Only the fact that he had let her escape him; that, on his way to her, he had been caught up in a strange fate as by a wind, had been borne off into other places, into other years, into another existence.

He visited Pauline for the last time. Her trunks remained half-full and still open in her room. She was at last *en route* for Dresden. Tunda talked with her father. M. Cardillac sat in an armchair which could not quite contain him; he jutted out over the seat and the arms although he was neither too fleshy nor too fat, muscular rather than portly, stocky rather than colossal. He was short, he stood firmly planted on short legs, unshakeable like an object made of iron; his nape was red and firm, his neck short, his hands broad, but his fingers – as if he had had them made as an afterthought – possessed a certain gracefulness. They made him almost likeable when they drummed on the table like naughty children, or fiddled with his waistcoat buttons or inserted themselves between neck and collar to ease the stiff edge of a shirt. Yes, Tunda even found M. Cardillac bearable. On the whole, he found it easier to tolerate the older generation; a son of M. Cardillac he would have found unbearable. But the father still suggested – when he momentarily forgot himself and became vulnerable – the endearing, honest, sympathy-evoking poverty of the working man, which is equivalent to open-mindedness and approximates to goodness. His simple honesty was buried, but still perceptible, under a layer of superimposed manners, hard-won and rigorously maintained inhibitions, under laboriously stratified defence-works of pride, self-assurance and imitated vanity. But when one looked M. Cardillac in the eye – he wore glasses, not because he was long-sighted but to mask his natural expression, and his brows projected over them – if, as it were, one removed these glasses with an intimate gaze and thus stripped M. Cardillac of his defences – then it came to pass that he began to speak of his hard youth in a gentle voice, lying only a little. But whenever the discussion turned to generalities Cardillac became formal, as if he had a mandate to represent that society of which he was a pillar and which was responsible for his comfortable position.

So Tunda conversed with M. Cardillac; he was even a little melancholy at having to leave his house. Cardillac invited him to return in the winter. He was in the habit of giving small, occasionally quite large, but usually intimate soirées at which young men were always welcome. They shook hands, Tunda accepted a cheque, took his leave of Mlle. Pauline and departed.

There was a car at the front door, the motor was still running, the chauffeur opened the door and a woman stepped out. She was slender, blonde, dressed in grey. Tunda noted at a glance her narrow shoes of smooth grey leather, evenly clasping her feet, the thin stockings with their bloom, an artificial and doubly provocative second skin, he clasped with both eyes, as if with both hands, the slender lissom hips. The woman came closer, and although it was barely three steps from the pavement-edge to the threshold where he stood, it seemed to him as if her passage lasted an eternity, as if she was coming to him, straight to him and not to the house, and as if he had been awaiting this woman on this spot for years.

Yes, she came nearer, he looked at her beautiful,

proud, beloved face. She returned his gaze. She looked at him, a little ruefully, a little flattered, as women look into a mirror they pass in a restaurant or on the stairs, happy to confirm their beauty and at the same time despising the cheapness of the glass which is incapable of reproducing it. Irene saw Tunda and did not recognize him. There was a wall in the depths of her gaze, a wall between retina and soul, a wall in her cool, grey, unwilling eyes.

Irene belonged to the other world. She was visiting the Cardillacs. She was accompaning Mlle. Pauline to Dresden. She lived a healthy and happy life, played golf, bathed by sandy beaches, had a rich husband, gave parties and attended them, belonged to charitable societies, and had a warm heart. But she did not recognize Tunda.

XXXIII

Tunda received a bulky letter, the first letter at last from Baranowicz.

It had had a roundabout journey, had been forwarded from Berlin to George; it was a widely-travelled letter, it had taken three months to arrive. It seemed to have grown heavier in transit.

Baranowicz sent his thanks for the money, he was prepared to repay it, and more besides. For he had made some excellent deals; the State had purchased part of his land, the ground contained valuable minerals. There was talk of platinum. Furthermore, in six months a new scientific expedition would be setting out through the *taiga* with Baranowicz as guide. If he so wished, Tunda could accompany him. Baranowicz had already received an advance for all kinds of equipment.

Then came a passage which took Tunda somewhat by surprise. It read :

I have almost forgotten the most important matter. Three months ago a woman arrived here – the thaw had started and the days were longer – a woman like a bird. She introduced herself as my sister-in-law, she came from the Caucasus with many furs and your photograph as evidence; three weeks it had taken her. A fur-trader from Omsk brought her. She said you had sent her money, And she came to me because I was the only relative she had in the world – her uncle, a potter, had died.

Her name is Alja and she is silent the greater part of the day.

I allowed her to stay, made her a bed, and so now she lives with me. We rarely talk and I don't ask her what she intends to do without you. She speaks very bad Russian whenever she does open her mouth.

By my standards, she is beautiful.

I can manage to give her money, if you want her to come to you. But I can also keep her here. It's all the same to me ! Write to me, *poste restante* at Irkutsk. Isaak Gorin, the gramophone dealer, brings my mail every month.

I have also bought a gramophone from him, and the woman who claims to be your wife often listens to it. Sometimes she cries, too. Maybe she cries because of you, I think to myself, and tears come to my eyes also.

I once thought of bringing Ekaterina Pavlovna

here, but she won't come. She has saved some money. She says she doesn't want to die among wolves, but in the town, among human beings.

So Tunda could go back to Baranowicz, whom he had left to seek Irene.

He could go back. His wife was already waiting for him.

He saw his brother's farmstead, the two dogs, Barin and Jegor, the great copper cauldron in which the meat cooked, the elk-skins on the low bed, he heard the striking of the clock, and the faint groan it emitted before each stroke, and the sharp rapping of the raven's beak on the window-sill.

But he did not yearn for the *taiga*. It seemed to him that his place and his destiny were here. He lived in an odour of corruption and fed on rottenness, he breathed the dust of the disintegrating houses and listened with delight to the song of the woodworms.

He still had Irene's photograph, exactly as he had carried it for years. It lay on his breast. It accompanied him through the streets. He stood there on the Place de la Madeleine, and looked down the Rue Royale.

That was when I met Tunda.

XXXIV

It was August 27th, 1926, at four in the afternoon. The shops were full, women crowded the department stores, models gyrated in the fashion salons, idlers gossiped in the confectioners, the wheels span in the factories, beggars deloused themselves on the banks of the Seine, loving couples embraced in the Bois de Boulogne, children played on the roundabouts in the public gardens. It was at this hour that my friend Tunda, thirty-two years of age, healthy and vigorous, a strong young man of diverse talents, stood on the Place de la Madeleine, in the centre of the capital of the world, without any idea what to do. He had no occupation, no desire, no hope, no ambition, and not even any self-love.

No one in the whole world was as superfluous as he.